Atlas for
The Great War

Thomas E. Griess
Series Editor

AVERY PUBLISHING GROUP INC.
Wayne, New Jersey

ISBN 0-89529-30

Contents

Foreword

Since the 1920's cadets at the United States Military Academy have studied the military campaigns of the First World War in varying degrees of detail. In 1938, T. Dodson Stamps, Head of the Department of Military Art and Engineering, initiated the development of a series of atlases to accompany historical narratives of various wars. Ultimately, the Department introduced one such atlas which was specifically designed to support a departmentally-prepared text on World War I. Thus began the concept of a closely integrated narrative and graphical portrayal which has persisted in the teaching of military history at West Point to the present day.

In 1959, a second generation text, *The West Point Atlas of American Wars*, edited by Colonel Vincent J. Esposito, was adopted for use at the Military Academy. This unique text, which included coverage of the First World War, served its purpose well. But as a result of fundamental modifications made in the course in the history of the military art in the past ten years, it became necessary to develop a new text.

This atlas, which is designed to support the new text, *The Great War*, provides in a graphic way primarily strategic coverage of the major campaigns of the war. Both the text and the atlas were prepared by three officer-instructors of the Department of History: James B. Agnew, Clifton R. Franks, and William R. Griffiths. We are indebted to these officers for the care and meticulousness they exercised in devising imaginative ways to depict military history while preserving the historical accuracy and exploiting the format of previous atlases produced at West Point.

The Department is also indebted to Mr. Edward J. Krasnoborski and his assistants, Ms. Deanne Beckwith and Mr. George Giddings, for the drafting of maps. Mr. Krasnoborski, drawing upon his many years of experience with the compilation of atlases at West Point, not only suggested the use of innovative techniques but also supervised the entire drafting effort and performed the major share of the preparation of maps.

Thomas E. Griess
Series Editor

TABLE OF SYMBOLS

BASIC SYMBOLS

Regiment III

Brigade x

Division xx

Corps xxx

Army xxxx

Army Group xxxxx

Infantry ....

Cavalry ....

Cavalry Covering Force .... • • • • • • •

Artillery ....

Artillery In Position ....
(Does not indicate type or quantity)

Trains ....

EXAMPLES OF COMBINATIONS OF BASIC SYMBOLS

Small infantry detachment ....

Third Reserve Division 3R

Canadian Corps .... CAN.

Fifth Cavalry Corps with other Units attached ...... V (+)

Debeney's French First Army .... FR. FIRST
DEBENEY

OTHER SYMBOLS

Actual location   Prior location

Troops on the march ....

Troops in position ....

Troops in bivouac or reserve ....

Troops displacing and direction ....

Troops in position under attack ....

Route of march .... ▪ ▪ ▶ ▪ ▪ ▶ ▪ ▪ ▶ ▪ ▪

Strong prepared defenses ....

Battle sites ....

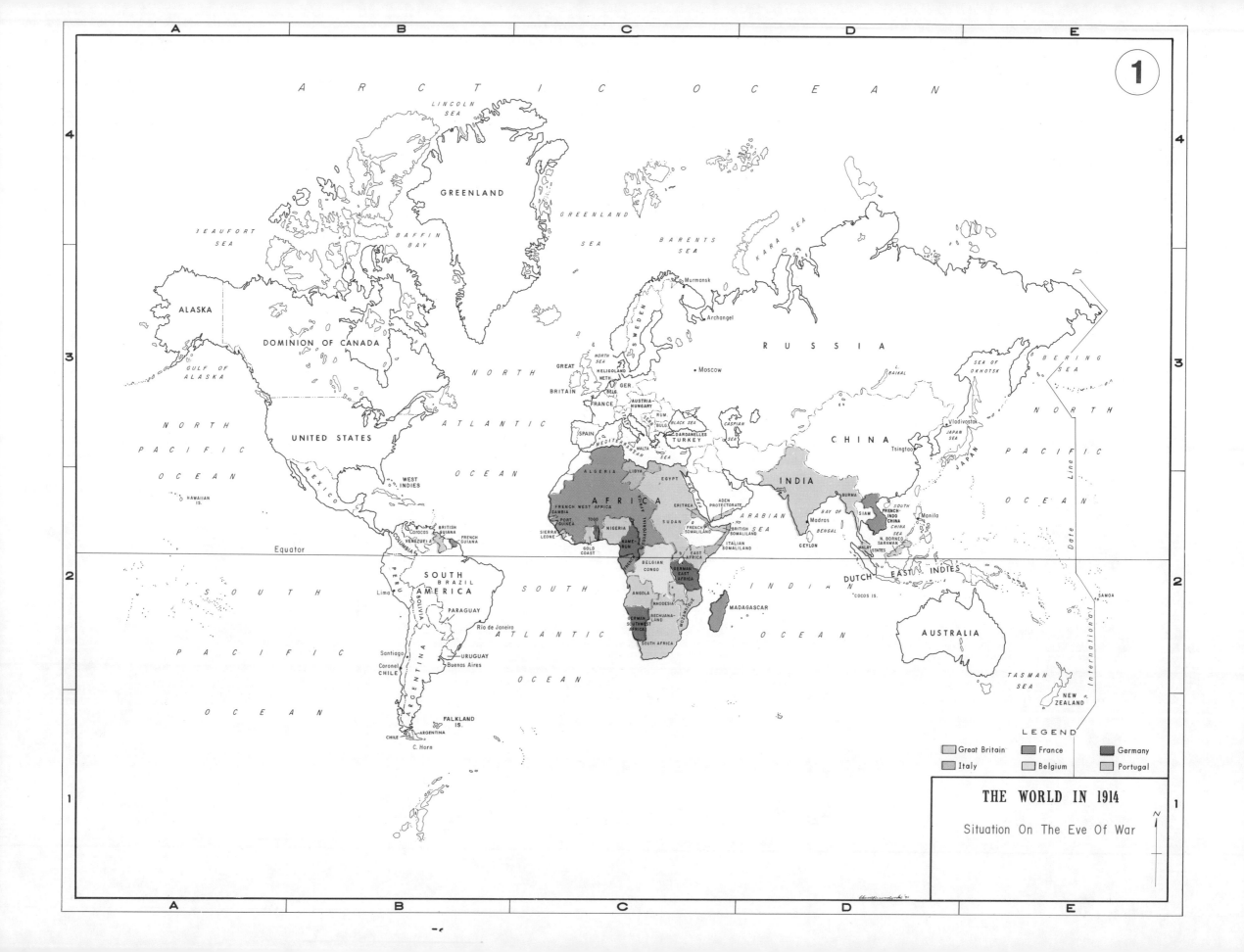

THE WORLD IN 1914

Situation On The Eve Of War

LEGEND

Great Britain | France | Germany
Italy | Belgium | Portugal

EUROPE, 1914

Allied Powers
Central Powers
Neutral Powers
Principal Rail Lines

2

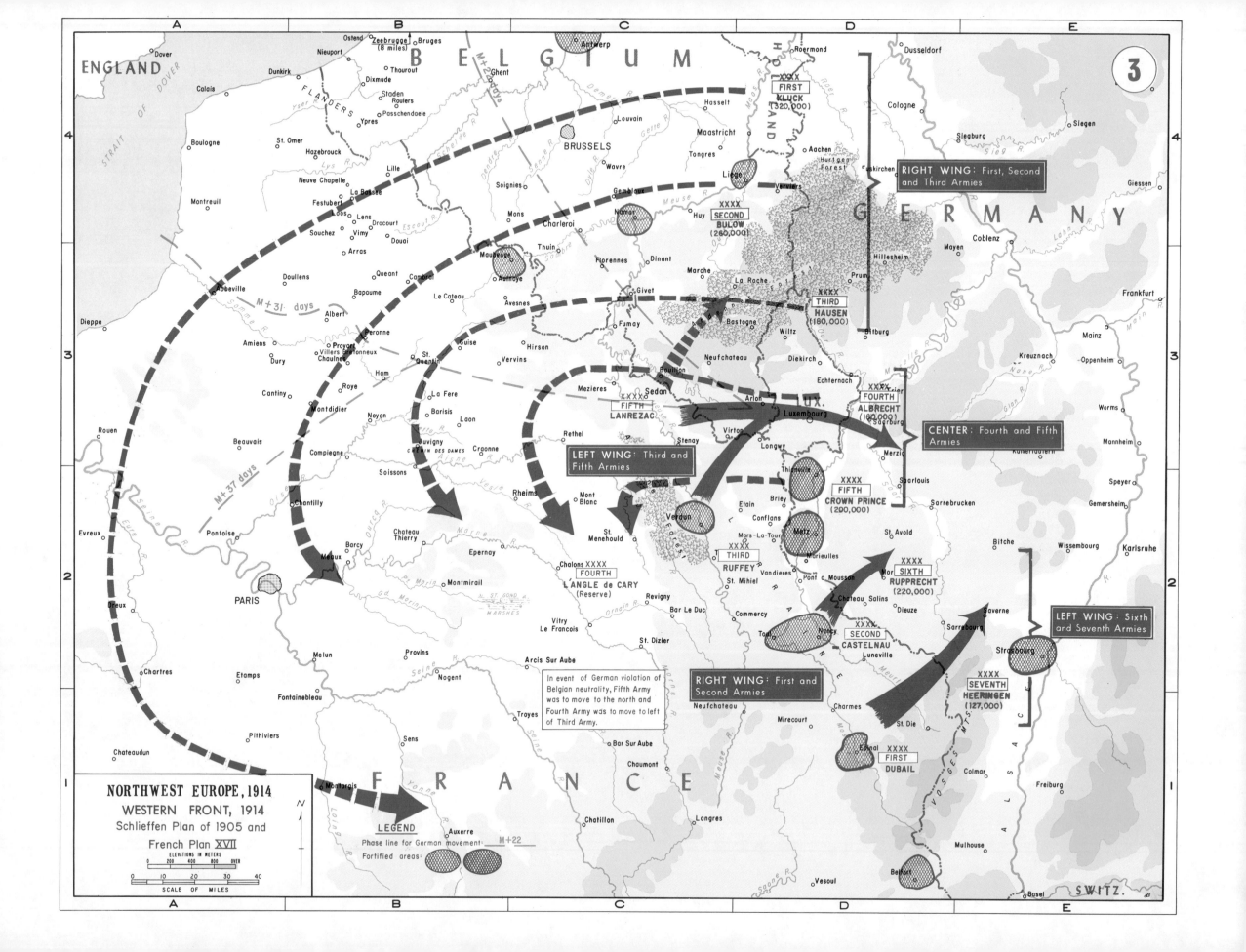

3

ENGLAND

B E L G I U M

BRUSSELS

XXXX
FIRST
KLUCK
(320,000)

RIGHT WING: First, Second
and Third Armies

G E R M A N Y

XXXX
SECOND
BULOW
(260,000)

XXXX
THIRD
HAUSEN
(180,000)

M + 22 days

M + 31 days

M + 37 days

XXXX
FIFTH
LANREZAC

XXXX
FOURTH
ALBRECHT
(180,000)

CENTER: Fourth and Fifth
Armies

LEFT WING: Third and
Fifth Armies

XXXX
FIFTH
CROWN PRINCE
(200,000)

PARIS

XXXX
FOURTH
L'ANGLE de CARY
(Reserve)

XXXX
THIRD
RUFFEY

XXXX
SIXTH
RUPPRECHT
(220,000)

LEFT WING: Sixth
and Seventh Armies

XXXX
SECOND
CASTELNAU

RIGHT WING: First and
Second Armies

In event of German violation of
Belgian neutrality, Fifth Army
was to move to the north and
Fourth Army was to move to left
of Third Army.

XXXX
SEVENTH
HEERINGEN
(127,000)

XXXX
FIRST
DUBAIL

F R A N C E

S W I T Z.

NORTHWEST EUROPE, 1914
WESTERN FRONT, 1914
Schlieffen Plan of 1905 and
French Plan XVII

ELEVATIONS IN METERS
0   200   400   800   OVER

0   10   20   30   40
SCALE OF MILES

LEGEND
Phase line for German movement: M + 22
Fortified areas:

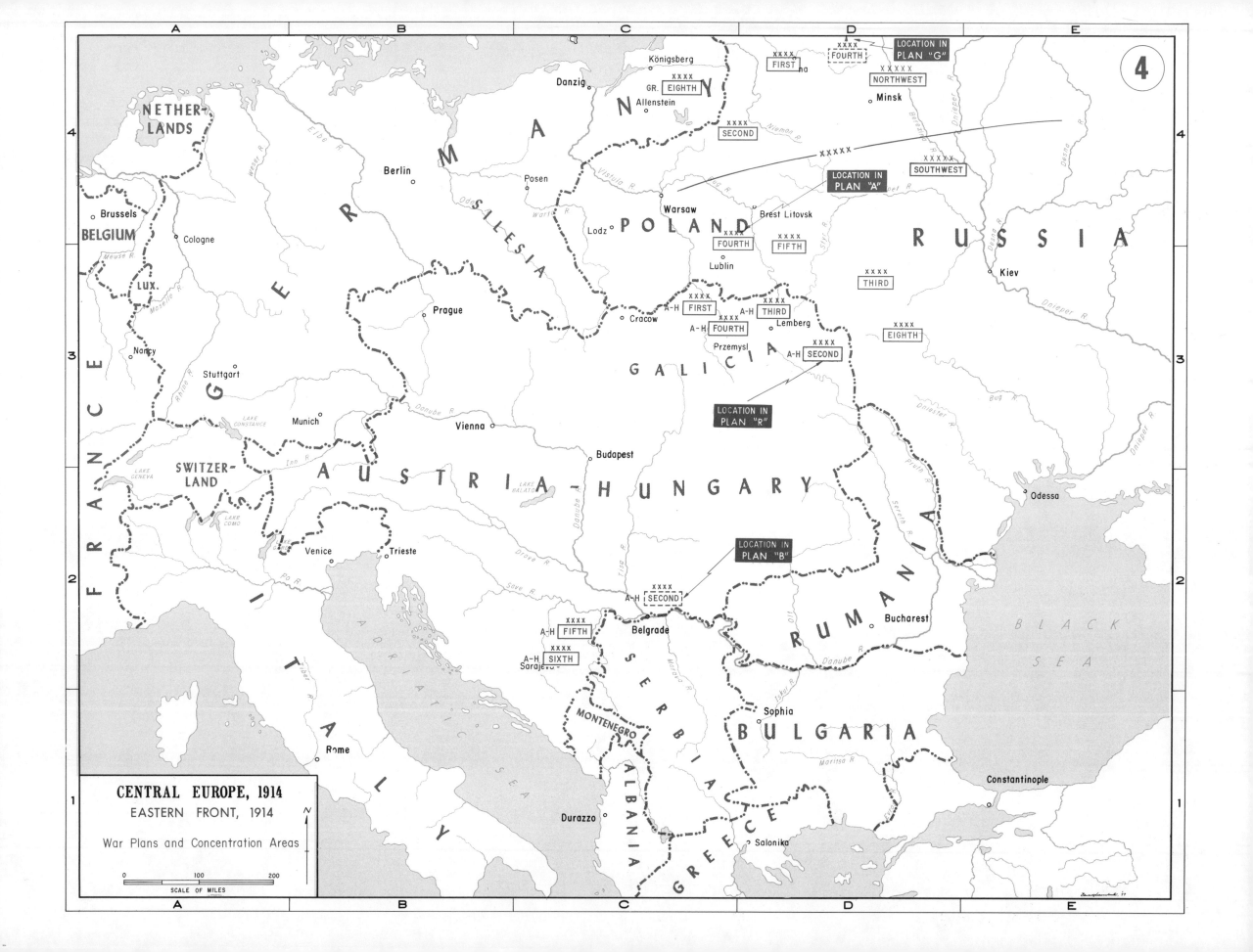

4

NETHER-
LANDS

Königsberg

Danzig

```
            xxxx
    GR. EIGHTH
```

Allenstein

```
   xxxx
  FIRST na
```

```
   xxxx
  FOURTH
```

LOCATION IN
PLAN "G"

NORTHWEST

Minsk

BELGIUM

Brussels

Cologne

LUX.

Nancy

Berlin

Posen

```
   xxxx
  SECOND
```

Warsaw

Brest Litovsk

```
   xxxx
  FOURTH
```

```
   xxxx
  FIFTH
```

LOCATION IN
PLAN "A"

SOUTHWEST

RUSSIA

Kiev

Lodz

Lublin

```
   xxxx
  THIRD
```

Stuttgart

Munich

Prague

Cracow

```
A-H  xxxx
    FIRST
```

```
A-H  xxxx
    THIRD
```

Lemberg

Przemysl

```
A-H  xxxx
    FOURTH
```

```
A-H  xxxx
    SECOND
```

```
   xxxx
  EIGHTH
```

GALICIA

GERMANY

SILESIA

POLAND

FRANCE

SWITZER-
LAND

LAKE
CONSTANCE

LAKE
GENEVA

LAKE
COMO

Vienna

Budapest

LOCATION IN
PLAN "R"

AUSTRIA-HUNGARY

LAKE
BALATON

Venice

Trieste

ITALY

LOCATION IN
PLAN "B"

```
A-H  xxxx
    SECOND
```

Bucharest

RUMANIA

Odessa

```
A-H  xxxx
    FIFTH
```

Belgrade

```
A-H  xxxx
    SIXTH
```

Sarajevo

SERBIA

MONTENEGRO

Rome

Durazzo

ALBANIA

Sophia

BULGARIA

BLACK
SEA

GREECE

Salonika

Constantinople

ADRIATIC SEA

CENTRAL EUROPE, 1914

EASTERN FRONT, 1914

War Plans and Concentration Areas

0   100   200

SCALE OF MILES

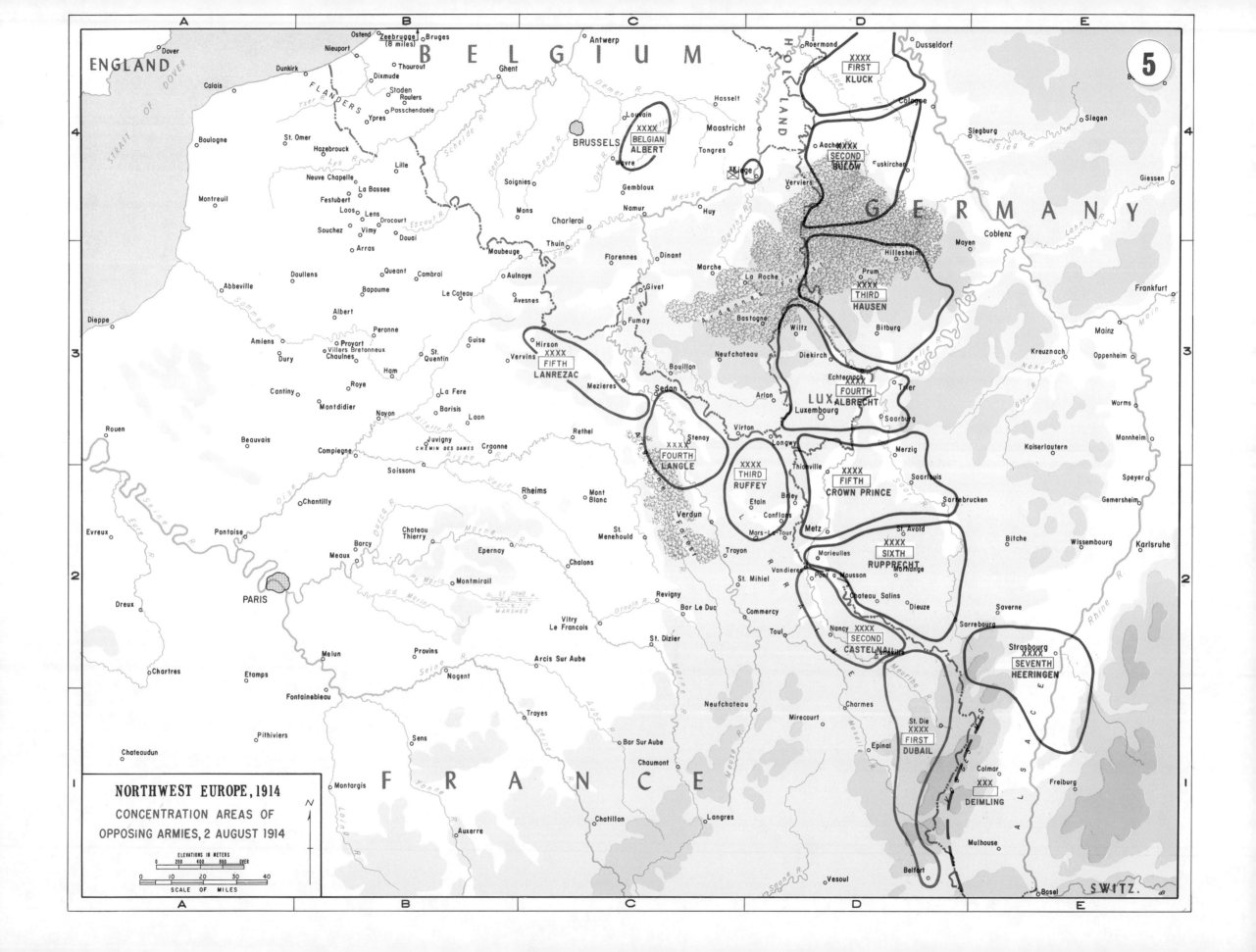

NORTHWEST EUROPE, 1914

CONCENTRATION AREAS OF
OPPOSING ARMIES, 2 AUGUST 1914

ELEVATIONS IN METERS

0 200 400 800 OVER

0   10   20   30   40
SCALE OF MILES

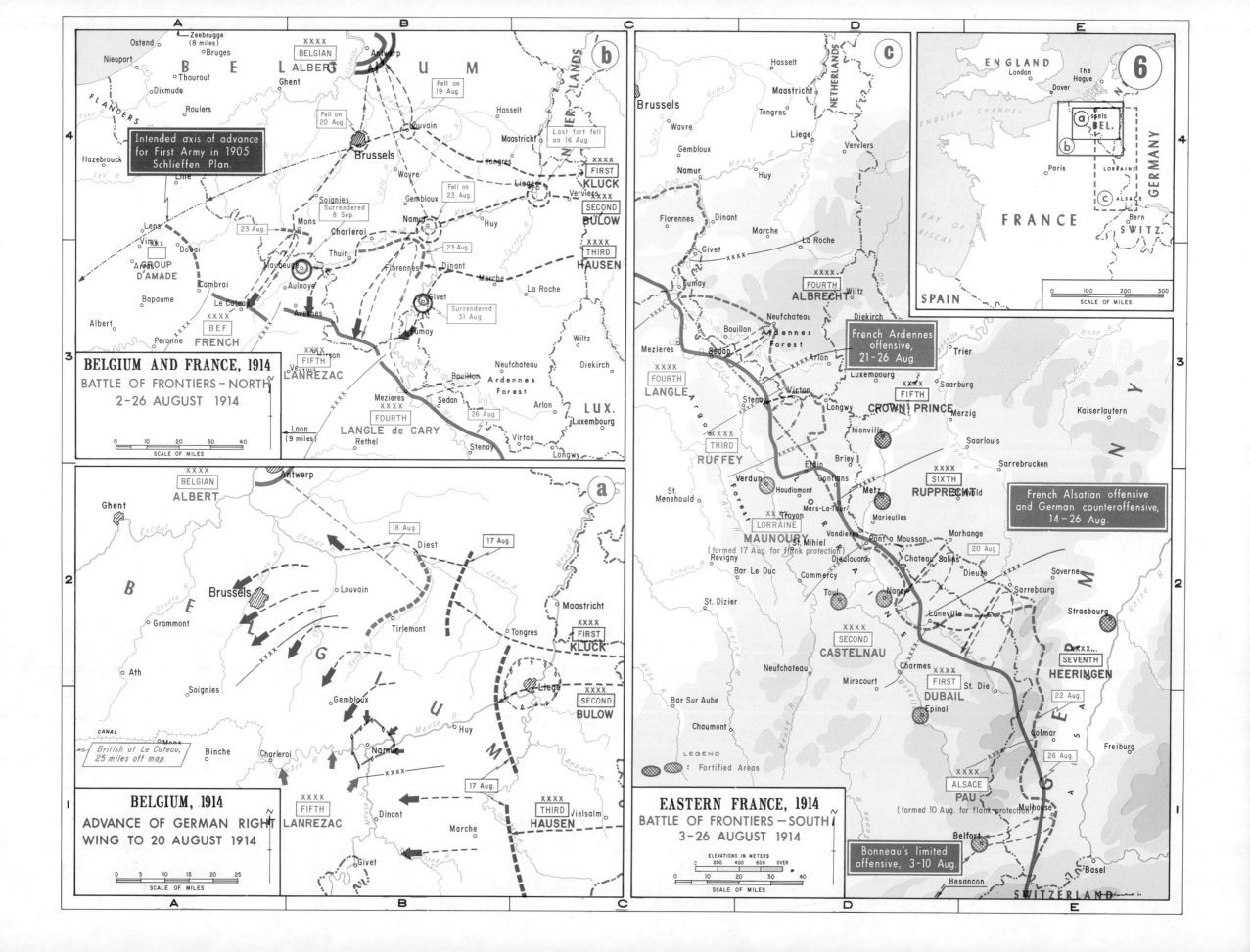

Map b — BELGIUM AND FRANCE, 1914 / BATTLE OF FRONTIERS—NORTH / 2-26 AUGUST 1914

ⓑ

NETHERLANDS

Ostend
Zeebrugge (8 miles)
Bruges
Nieuport
Thourout
Dixmude
Roulers
FLANDERS
Yser R.
Hazebrouck
Lys R.
Lille
Lens
Vimy
Douai
GROUP D'AMADE
Arras
Bapaume
Albert
Peronne
Cambrai
Le Cateau
Avesnes

XXXX BELGIAN ALBERT
Antwerp
Ghent
Scheldt R.

Intended axis of advance for First Army in 1905 Schlieffen Plan.

Fell on 20 Aug.
Louvain
Fell on 19 Aug.
Brussels
Wavre
Gembloux
Dyle R.
Soignies
Surrendered 8 Sep.
Mons
23 Aug.
Charleroi
Thuin
Maubeuge
Aulnoye
Namur
Sambre R.
Fell on 23 Aug.
Huy
Liege
Verviers
Last fort fell on 16 Aug.
Hasselt
Maastricht
Tongres

XXXX FIRST KLUCK
XXXX SECOND BULOW
XXXX THIRD HAUSEN

23 Aug.
Florennes
Dinant
Givet
Surrendered 31 Aug.
Fumay
Marche
La Roche
Wiltz
Meuse R.

XXXX BEF FRENCH
XXXX FIFTH LANREZAC
Mezieres
Sedan
Bouillon
Neufchateau
Ardennes Forest
Arlon
Diekirch
LUX.

XXXX FOURTH LANGLE de CARY
Laon (9 miles)
Rethel
Virton
Stenay
Longwy
Luxembourg
26 Aug.

SCALE OF MILES 0 10 20 30 40

Map a — BELGIUM, 1914 / ADVANCE OF GERMAN RIGHT WING TO 20 AUGUST 1914

ⓐ

Antwerp
XXXX BELGIAN ALBERT
Ghent
Escaut R.
Dendre R.
18 Aug.
Diest
Demer R.
17 Aug.
Brussels
Louvain
Grammont
Gette R.
Ath
Soignies
Tirlemont
Tongres
Maastricht
XXXX FIRST KLUCK

CANAL
British at Le Cateau, 25 miles off map.
Mons
Binche
Charleroi
Gembloux
Sambre R.
Namur
Meuse R.
Huy
Liege
XXXX SECOND BULOW

XXXX FIFTH LANREZAC
Dinant
Marche
Givet
17 Aug.
Vielsalm
Ambleve R.
XXXX THIRD HAUSEN

SCALE OF MILES 0 5 10 15 20 25

Map c — EASTERN FRANCE, 1914 / BATTLE OF FRONTIERS—SOUTH / 3-26 AUGUST 1914

ⓒ

NETHERLANDS
Brussels
Hasselt
Maastricht
Tongres
Liege
Gembloux
Namur
Verviers
Gette R.
Meuse R.
Ourthe R.
Florennes
Dinant
Marche
La Roche
Givet
Fumay
Mezieres
Sedan
Bouillon
Ardennes Forest
Neufchateau
Arlon
Diekirch
Luxembourg
Wiltz

XXXX FOURTH ALBRECHT
French Ardennes offensive, 21-26 Aug.
XXXX FOURTH LANGLE
XXXX THIRD RUFFEY
Argonne Forest
Stenay
Virton
Longwy
XXXX FIFTH CROWN PRINCE
Trier
Saarburg
Merzig
Kaiserlautern

Verdun
Haudiomont
Conflans
Briey
Etain
Thionville
Metz
Mars-La-Tour
Marieulles
XXXX SIXTH RUPPRECHT
Saarlouis
Sarrebrucken
St. Menehould
Troyon
St. Mihiel
Vandieres
Pont a Mousson
Chateau Salins
Morhange
20 Aug.
Dieuze
Sarrebourg
Saverne
Strasbourg

LORRAINE
MAUNOURY
(formed 17 Aug. for flank protection)
Revigny
Bar Le Duc
Commercy
Dieulouard
Nancy
Luneville
French Alsatian offensive and German counteroffensive, 14-26 Aug.

XXXX SECOND CASTELNAU
Toul
Neufchateau
Mirecourt
Charmes
XXXX FIRST DUBAIL
St. Die
22 Aug.
Colmar
Freiburg
Rhine R.

Bar Sur Aube
Chaumont
Epinal
St. Dizier
Moselle R.
XXXX SEVENTH HEERINGEN

Meuse R.
Saone R.

LEGEND: Fortified Areas
Bonneau's limited offensive, 3-10 Aug.
XXXX ALSACE PAU
(formed 10 Aug. for flank protection)
Mulhouse
26 Aug.
Belfort
Basel
SWITZERLAND

ELEVATIONS IN METERS
200 400 600 OVER
SCALE OF MILES 0 10 20 30 40

Map 6 — inset

⑥

ENGLAND
London
Dover
The Hague
ENGLISH CHANNEL
BEL.
ⓐ
ⓑ
GERMANY
Paris
LORRAINE
ⓒ ALSACE
Bern
FRANCE
BAY OF BISCAY
SWITZ.
SPAIN

SCALE OF MILES 0 100 200 300

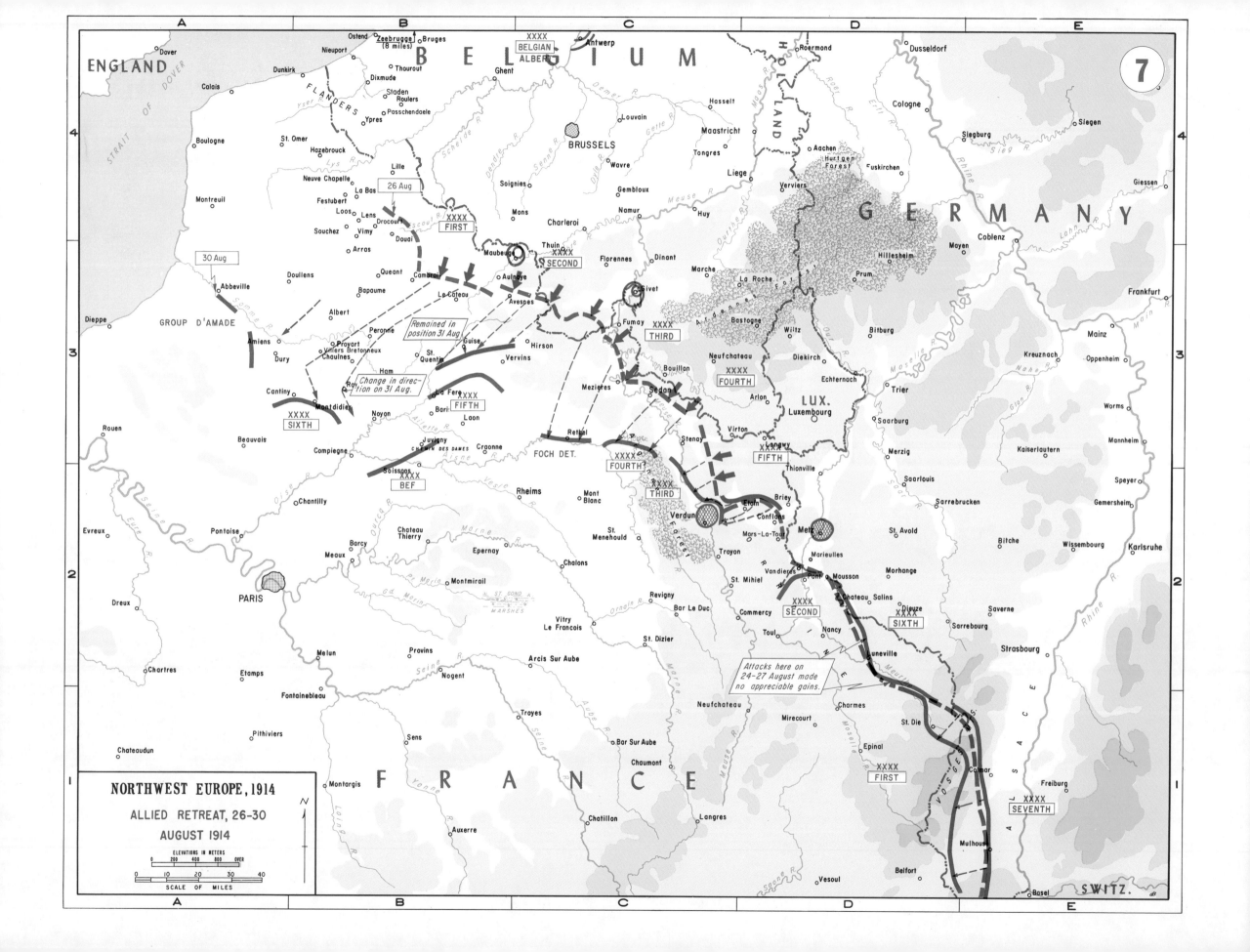

NORTHWEST EUROPE, 1914

ALLIED RETREAT, 26-30

AUGUST 1914

ELEVATIONS IN METERS
0   200   400   800   OVER

0   10   20   30   40
SCALE OF MILES

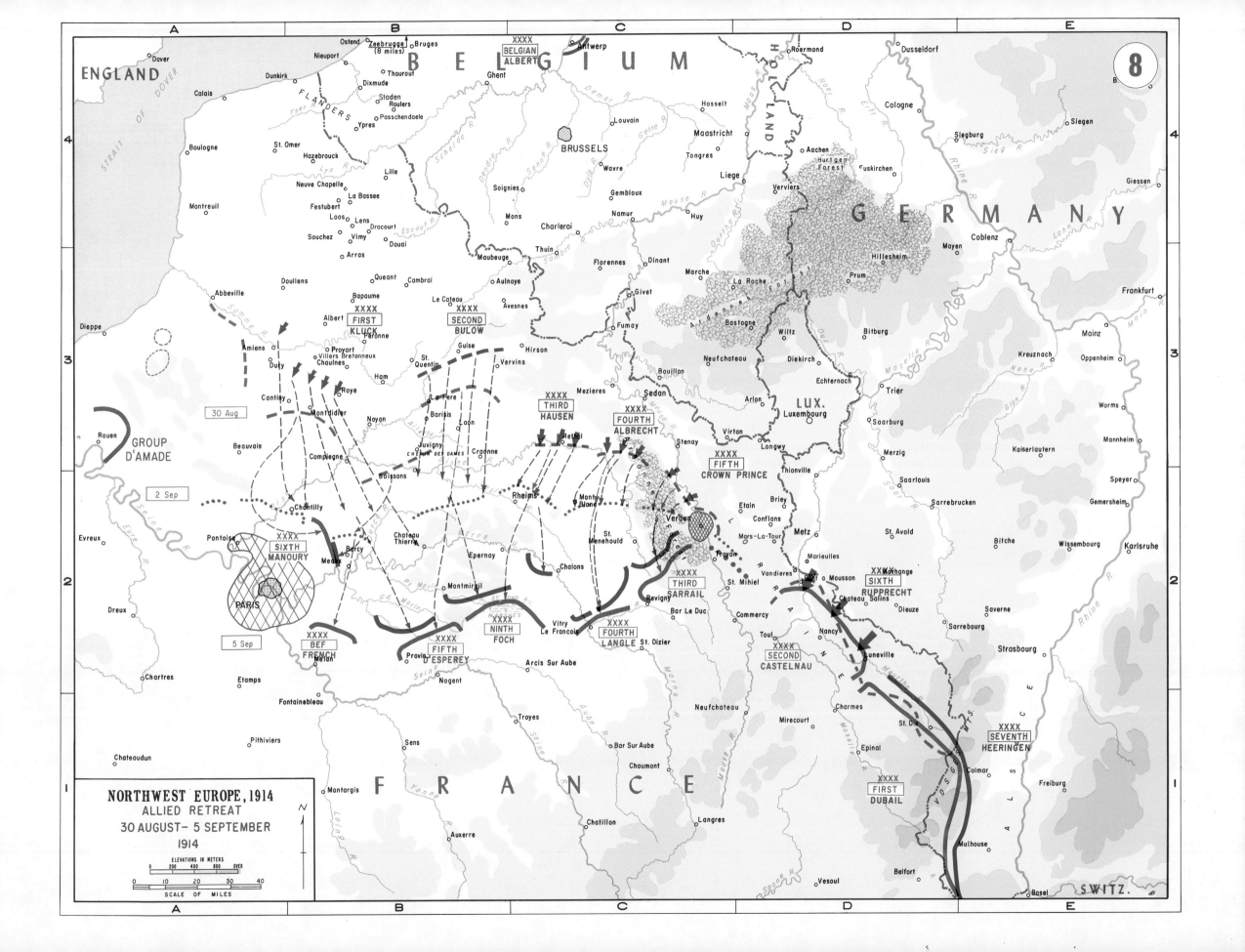

NORTHWEST EUROPE, 1914
ALLIED RETREAT
30 AUGUST - 5 SEPTEMBER
1914

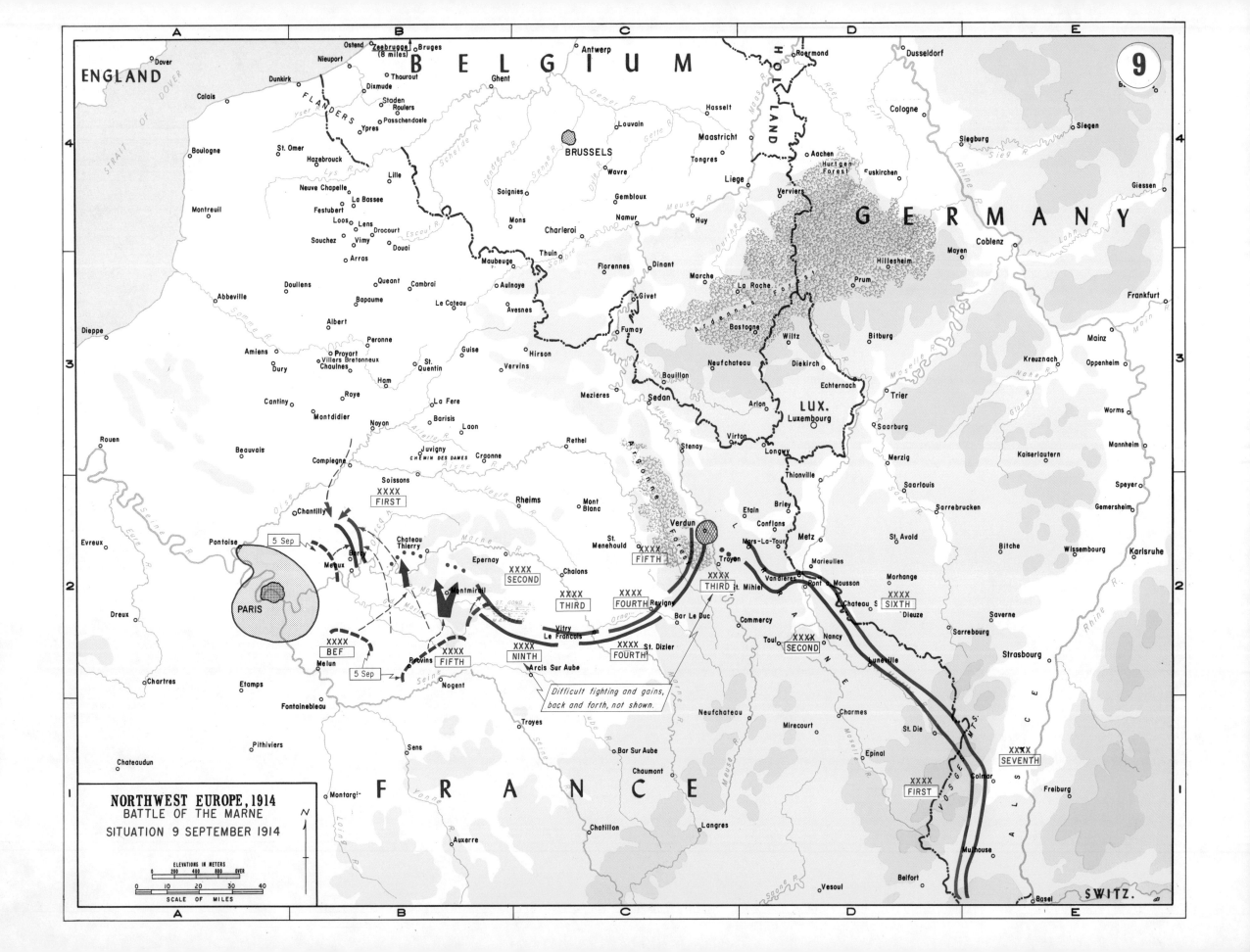

NORTHWEST EUROPE, 1914
BATTLE OF THE MARNE
SITUATION 9 SEPTEMBER 1914

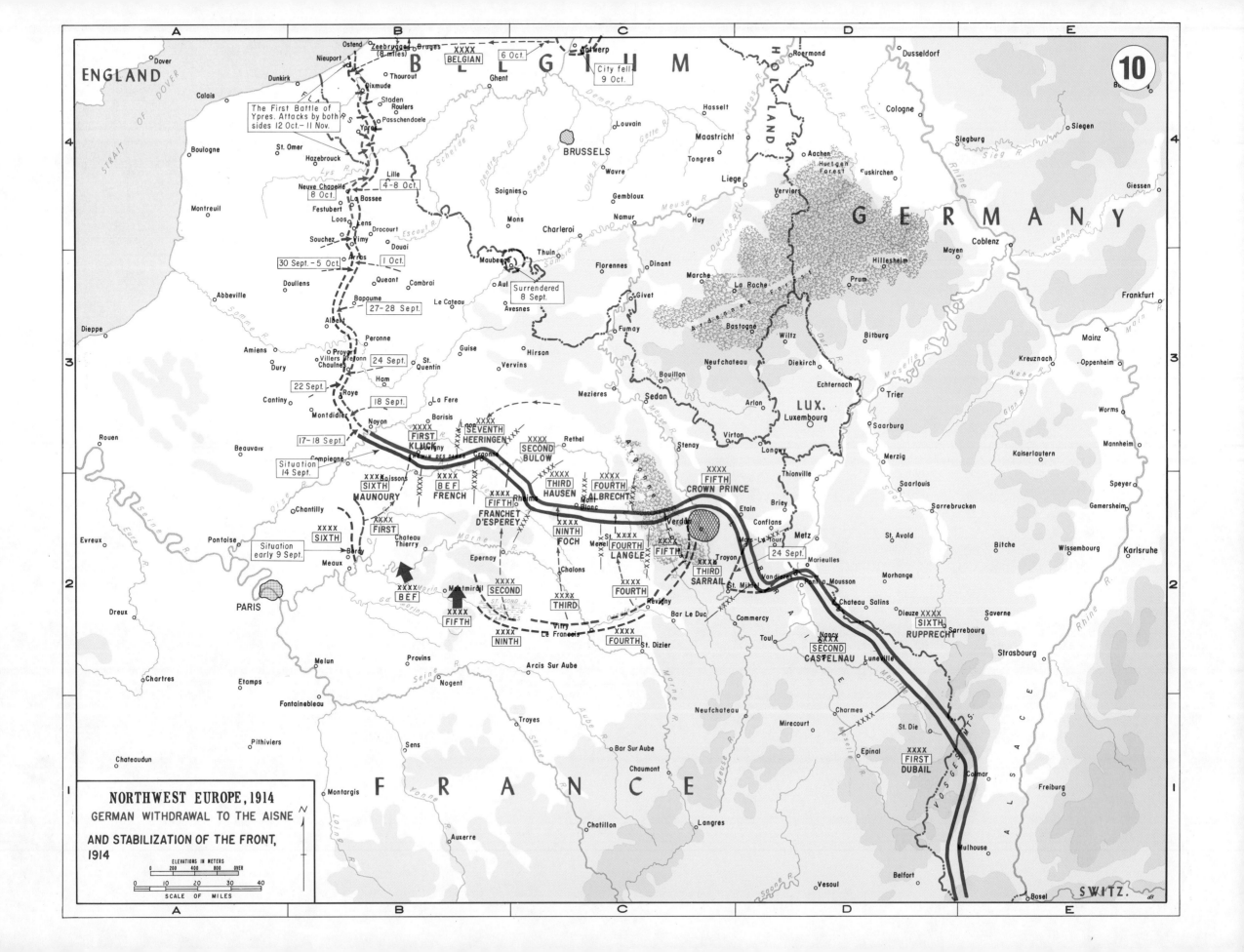

NORTHWEST EUROPE, 1914

GERMAN WITHDRAWAL TO THE AISNE

AND STABILIZATION OF THE FRONT, 1914

ELEVATIONS IN METERS
200   400   800   OVER

0   10   20   30   40
SCALE OF MILES

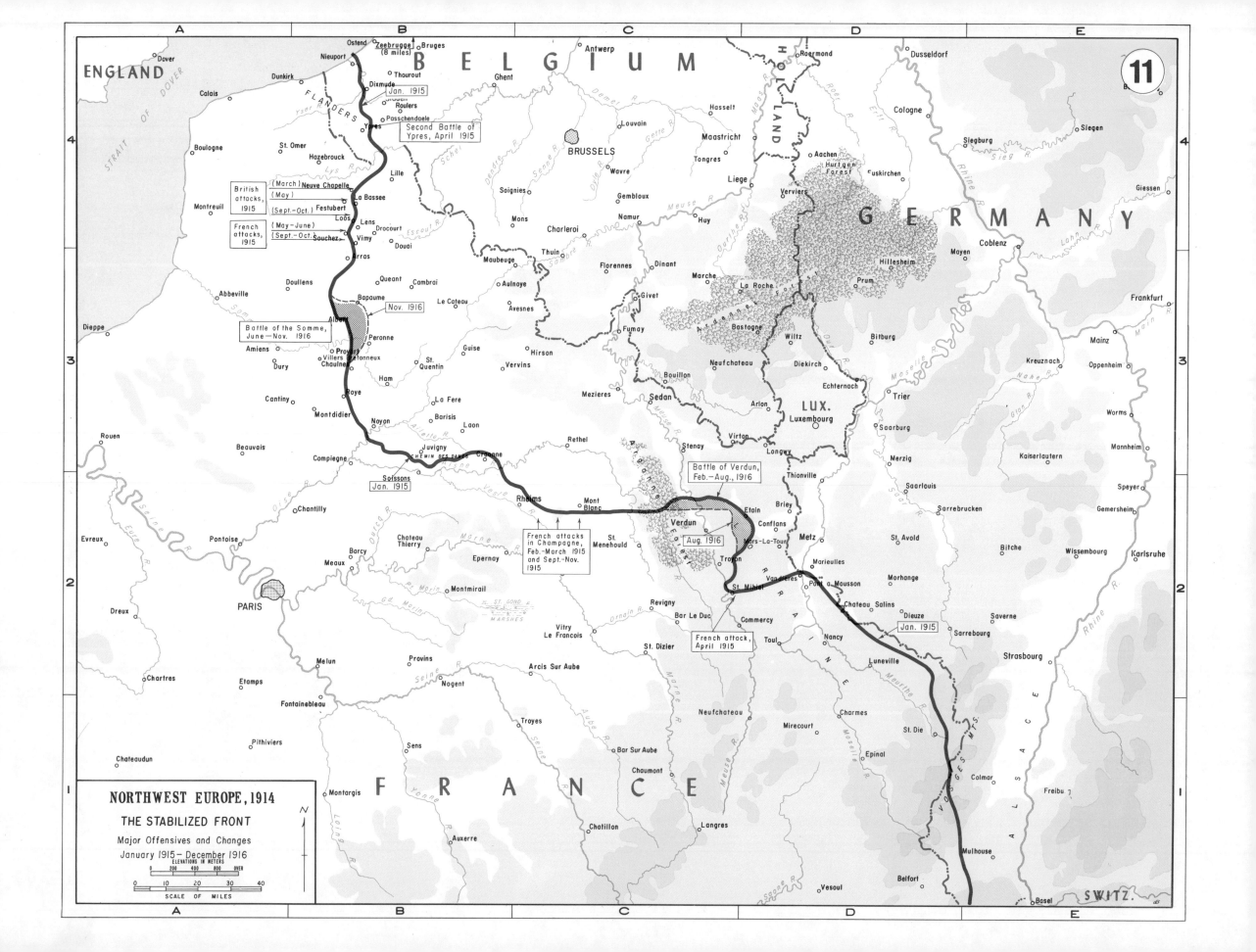

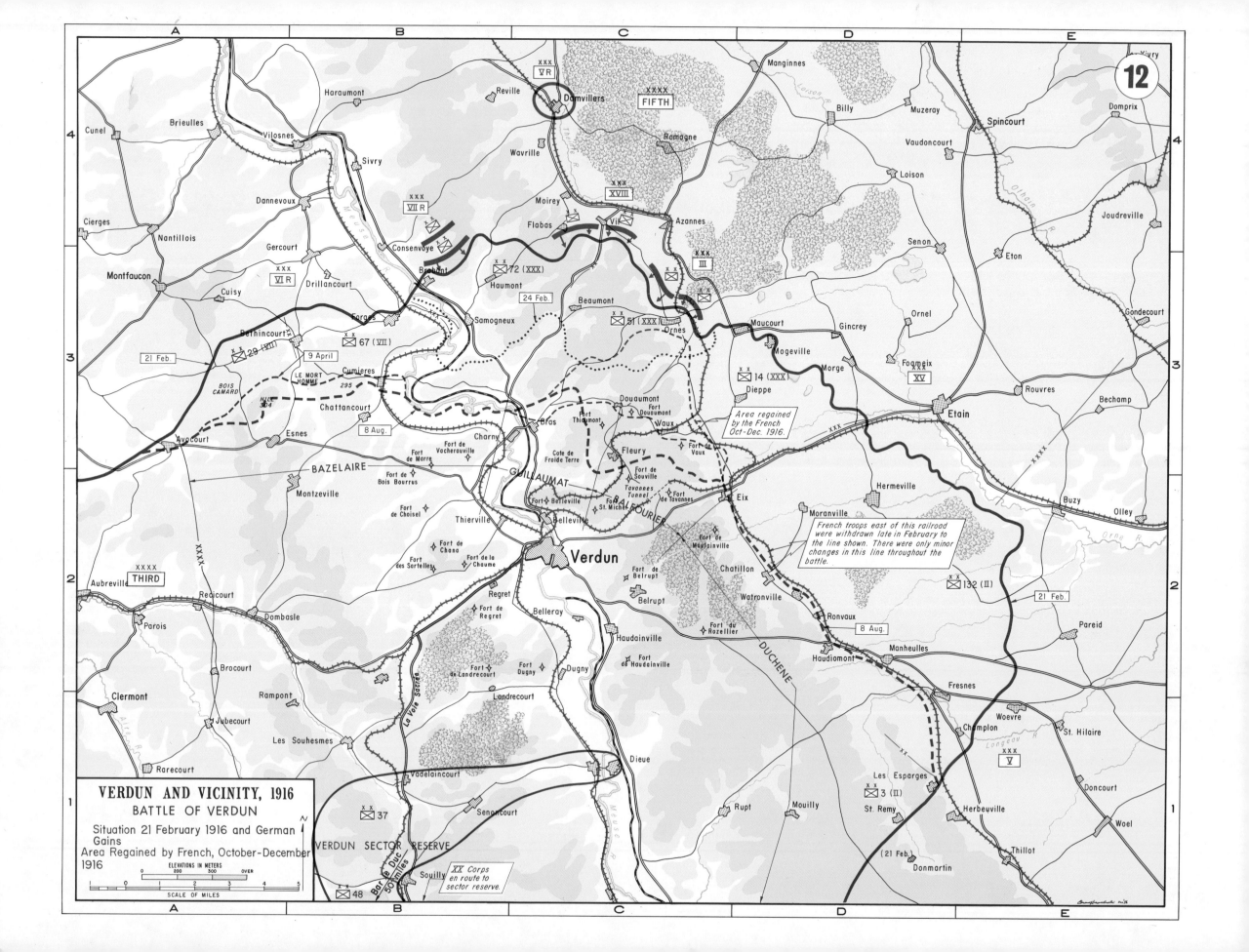

12

VERDUN AND VICINITY, 1916
BATTLE OF VERDUN

Situation 21 February 1916 and German Gains
Area Regained by French, October-December 1916

ELEVATIONS IN METERS

200   300   OVER

SCALE OF MILES

Area regained by the French Oct.-Dec. 1916.

French troops east of this railroad were withdrawn late in February to the line shown. There were only minor changes in this line throughout the battle.

XX Corps en route to sector reserve.

VERDUN SECTOR RESERVE

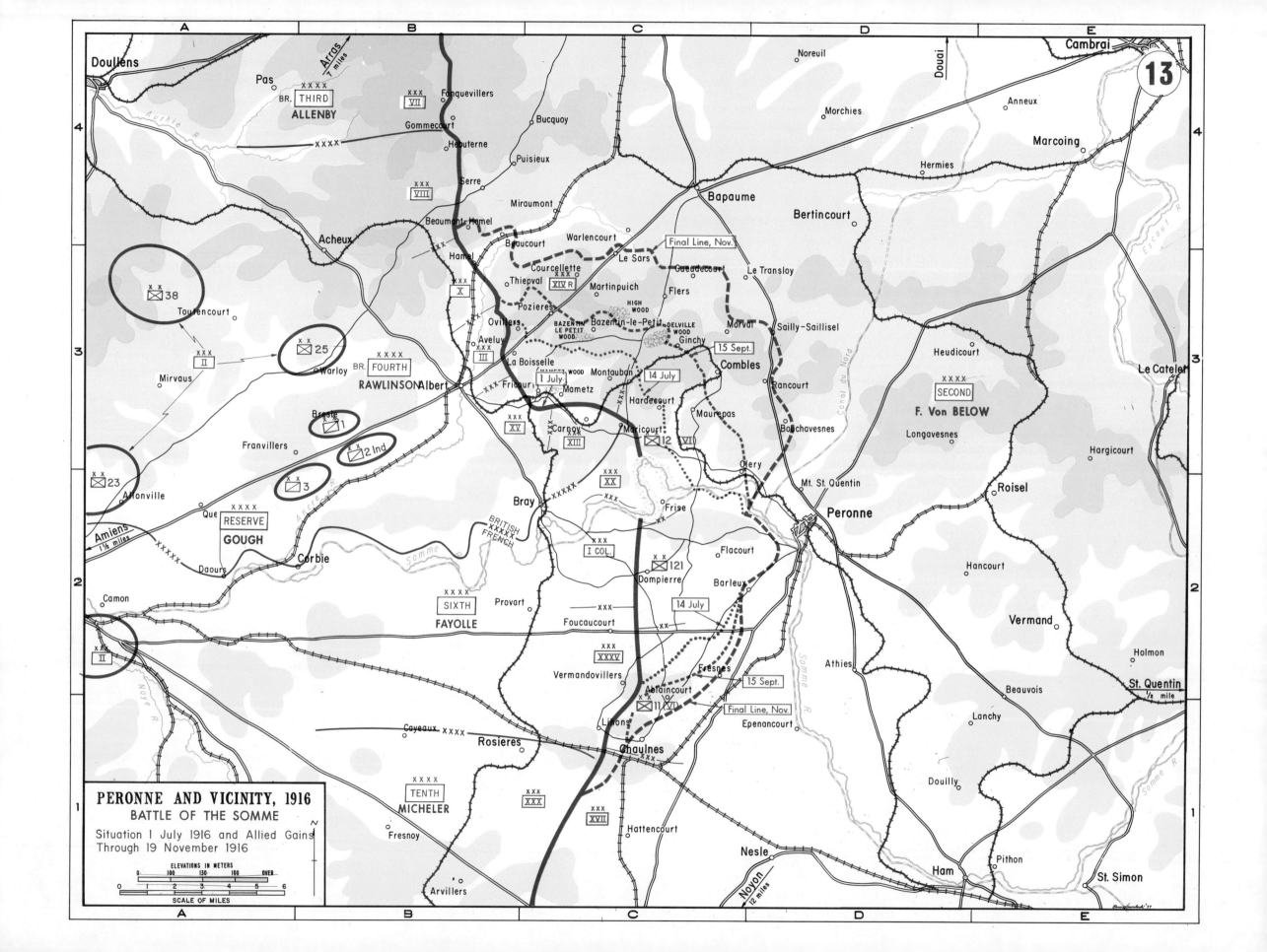

PERONNE AND VICINITY, 1916
BATTLE OF THE SOMME
Situation 1 July 1916 and Allied Gains
Through 19 November 1916

ELEVATIONS IN METERS
100   130   160   OVER
0   1   2   3   4   5   6
SCALE OF MILES

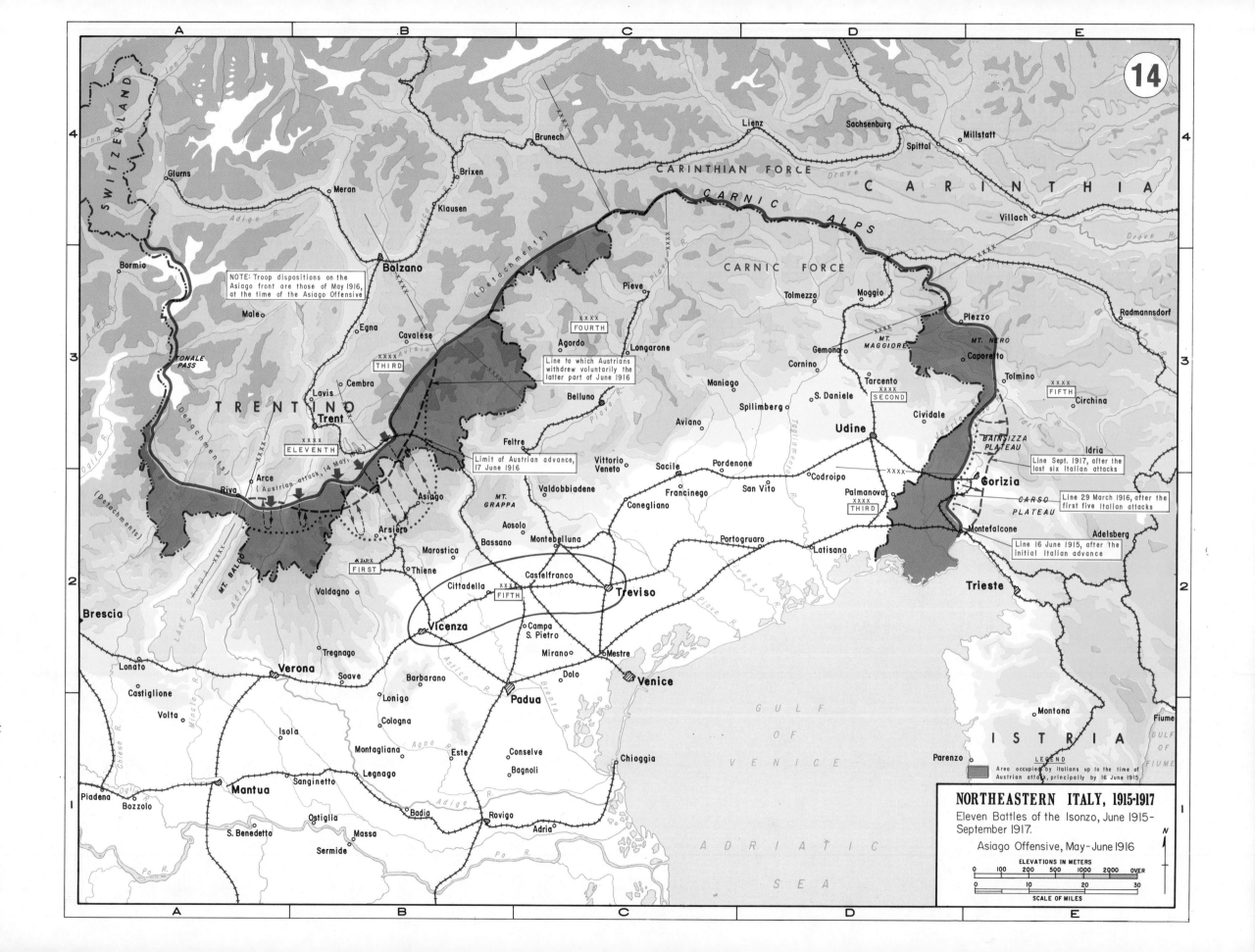

Map grid labels (top and bottom): A B C D E
Map grid labels (left and right): 4 3 2 1

14

SWITZERLAND

Inn R.

Glurns

Bormio

Male

TONALE
PASS

TRENTINO

Arce
(Austrian attack, 14 May)

Riva

MT. BALDO

Lonato

Verona

Castiglione

Volta

Brescia

Oglio R.

Chiese R.

Piadena

Bozzolo

S. Benedetto

Ostiglia

Sermide

Mantua

Sanginetto

Badia

Po R.

Meran

Klausen

Egna

Cavalese

Lavis

Cembra

Trent

XXXX
ELEVENTH

XXXX
THIRD

Avisio R.

Bolzano

Brixen

Brunech

Pieve

Agordo

Longarone

Belluno

Feltre

NOTE: Troop dispositions on the
Asiago front are those of May 1916,
at the time of the Asiago Offensive.

Line to which Austrians
withdrew voluntarily the
latter part of June 1916

Limit of Austrian advance,
17 June 1916

(Detachments)

(Detachments)

Piave R.

XXXX
FOURTH

CARNIC FORCE

CARNIC ALPS

CARINTHIAN FORCE

Lienz

Sachsenburg

Spittal

Millstatt

Drave R.

CARINTHIA

Villach

Radmannsdorf

Tolmezzo

Moggio

Gemona

Cornino

Maniago

S. Daniele

Spilimberg

MT.
MAGGIORE

Tarcento

XXXX
SECOND

Cividale

Plezzo

MT. NERO

Caporetto

Tolmino

XXXX
FIFTH

Circhina

Idria

BAINSIZZA
PLATEAU

Tagliamento R.

Judrio R.

Gorizia

CARSO
PLATEAU

Line Sept. 1917, after the
last six Italian attacks

Line 29 March 1916, after the
first five Italian attacks

Line 16 June 1915, after the
initial Italian advance

Udine

Aviano

Vittorio
Veneto

Sacile

Pordenone

Codroipo

Francinego

San Vito

Palmanova

XXXX
THIRD

Montefalcone

Adelsberg

Valdobbiadene

Conegliano

Portogruaro

Latisana

Livenza R.

Treviso

Mestre

ISTRIA

Montona

Fiume

GULF
OF
FIUME

Parenzo

Trieste

MT.
GRAPPA

Aosolo

Montebelluna

Casfelfranco

Campa
S. Pietro

Mirano

Dolo

Venice

GULF
OF
VENICE

Chioggia

ADRIATIC
SEA

Asiago

Arsiero

Marostica

Thiene

XXXX
FIRST

XXXX
FIFTH

Cittadella

Vicenza

Valdagno

Astico R.

Agno R.

Brenta R.

Padua

Adige R.

Tregnago

Soave

Barbarano

Lonigo

Cologna

Montagliana

Isola

Este

Legnago

Conselve

Bagnoli

Massa

Rovigo

Adria

Po R.

Bassano

LEGEND

Area occupied by Italians up to the time of
Austrian attack, principally by 16 June 1915

NORTHEASTERN ITALY, 1915-1917

Eleven Battles of the Isonzo, June 1915–
September 1917.

Asiago Offensive, May–June 1916

ELEVATIONS IN METERS

0 100 200 500 1000 2000 OVER

0 10 20 30

SCALE OF MILES

N

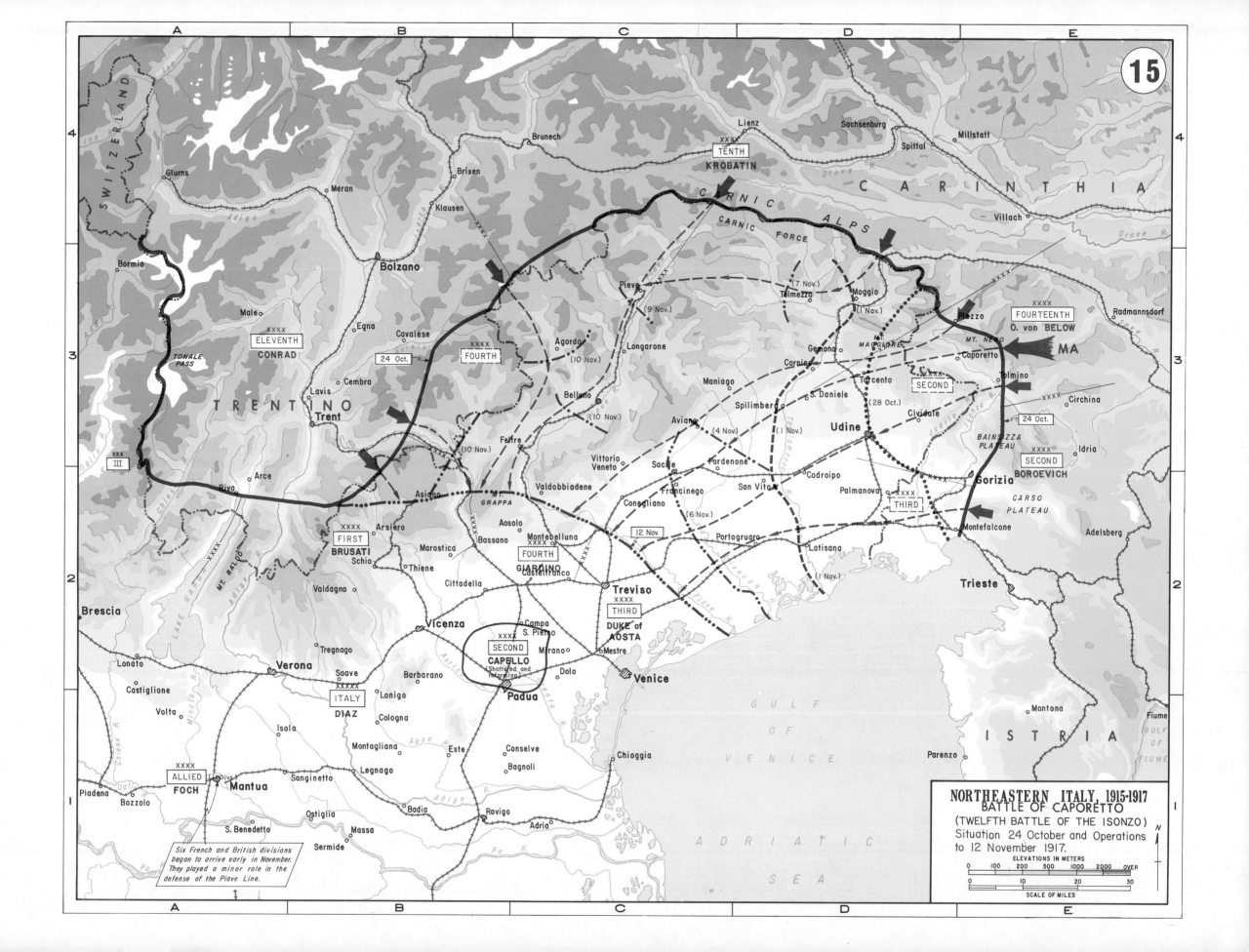

NORTHEASTERN ITALY, 1915-1917
BATTLE OF CAPORETTO
(TWELFTH BATTLE OF THE ISONZO)
Situation 24 October and Operations
to 12 November 1917.

ELEVATIONS IN METERS
0 100 200 500 1000 2000 OVER

SCALE OF MILES
0 10 20 30

Six French and British divisions
began to arrive early in November.
They played a minor role in the
defense of the Piave Line.

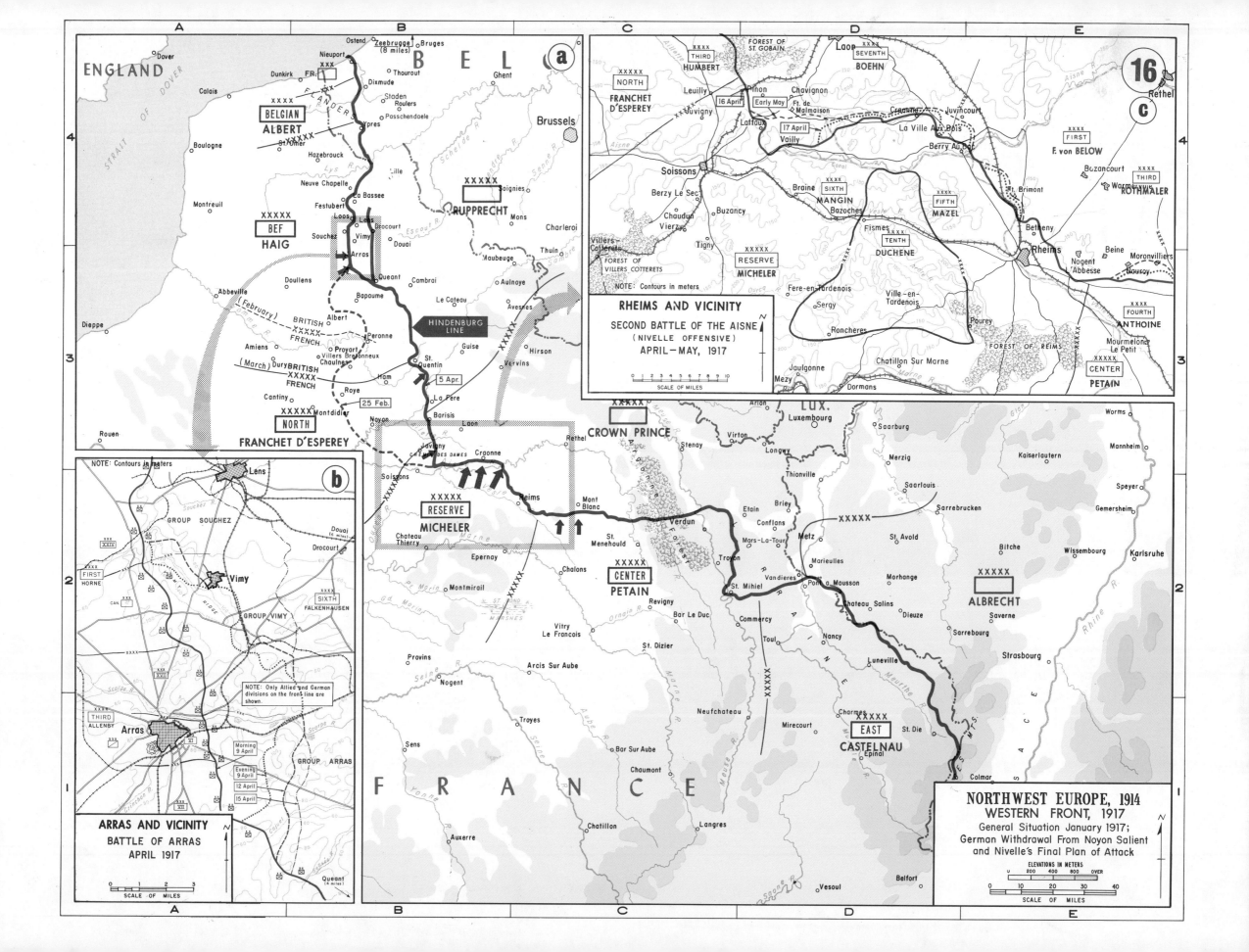

Map (a) — Main map, Northwest Europe:

ENGLAND

BELGIUM

FRANCE

LUX.

Dover, Calais, Boulogne, Montreuil, Abbeville, Dieppe, Rouen, Amiens

Ostend, Zeebrugge (8 miles), Bruges, Ghent, Brussels

Nieuport, Dixmude, Thourout, Staden, Roulers, Passchendaele, Ypres

FR. XXX
XXXX FLANDERS
BELGIAN
ALBERT
XXXXX

Dunkirk, St. Omer, Hazebrouck, Lille, Neuve Chapelle, La Bassee, Festubert, Loos, Lens, Douai

BEF
HAIG
XXXXX

Souchez, Vimy, Arras, Drocourt, Queant, Cambrai

RUPPRECHT
XXXXX

Soignies, Mons, Charleroi, Maubeuge, Thuin, Aulnoye, Avesnes, Le Cateau

HINDENBURG LINE

(February)
BRITISH XXXXX FRENCH

Doullens, Albert, Bapaume, Peronne, Proyart, Villers Bretonneux, Chaulnes, Ham, Roye

(March) BRITISH XXXXX FRENCH

Dury, Cantiny, Montdidier

NORTH
FRANCHET D'ESPEREY
XXXXX

St. Quentin, Guise, Hirson, Vervins, La Fere, Barisis, Noyon, Laon, Craonne

5 Apr., 25 Feb.

RESERVE
MICHELER
XXXXX

Juvigny, CHEMIN DES DAMES, Soissons, Reims, Mont Blanc, Chateau Thierry, Epernay, Chalons

CROWN PRINCE
XXXXX

Rethel, Arlon, Luxembourg, Virton, Stenay, Longwy, Thionville, Briey, Conflans, Etain

CENTER
PETAIN
XXXXX

Verdun, Mars-La-Tour, St. Mihiel, Troyon, St. Menehould, Revigny, Commercy, Bar Le Duc

Montmirail, Vitry Le Francois, St. Dizier, Chalons, Provins, Nogent, Arcis Sur Aube, Troyes, Sens

Metz, St. Avold, Morhange, Marieulles, Pont a Mousson, Vandieres, Chateau Salins, Dieuze

ALBRECHT
XXXXX

Saarburg, Saarlouis, Sarrebourg, Saverne, Bitche, Wissembourg, Karlsruhe, Strasbourg

Nancy, Luneville, Charmes, St. Die, Epinal, Colmar

EAST
CASTELNAU
XXXXX

Neufchateau, Mirecourt, Toul, Chaumont, Langres, Auxerre, Chatillon, Vesoul, Belfort, Worms, Mannheim, Merzig, Kaiserslautern, Gemersheim, Speyer

16

Inset (a) — RHEIMS AND VICINITY:

Laon, Soissons, Rheims, Rethel

THIRD HUMBERT
NORTH FRANCHET D'ESPEREY
SEVENTH BOEHN

Leuilly, Juvigny, Pinon, Chavignon, Ft. de Malmaison, Laffaux, Vailly, Craonne, Juvincourt, La Ville Aux Bois, Berry Au Bac

16 April, Early May, 17 April

SIXTH MANGIN
FIRST F. von BELOW
Buzancourt, Warmeriville, ROTHMALER

Berzy Le Sec, Braine, Buzancy, Bazoches, Chaudun, Vierzy, Tigny, Fismes

FIFTH MAZEL
THIRD

TENTH DUCHENE
Ft. Brimont, Betheny, Beine, Nogent l'Abbesse, Moronvilliers

RESERVE MICHELER
XXXXX

Fere-en-Tardenois, Sergy, Ville-en-Tardenois, Roncheres, Pourcy, Jaulgonne, Chatillon Sur Marne, Mezy, Dormans

FOURTH ANTHOINE
CENTER PETAIN
Mourmelon Le Petit
FOREST OF REIMS

NOTE: Contours in meters

RHEIMS AND VICINITY
SECOND BATTLE OF THE AISNE
(NIVELLE OFFENSIVE)
APRIL–MAY, 1917

0 1 2 3 4 5 6 7 8 9 10
SCALE OF MILES

c

Inset (b) — ARRAS AND VICINITY:

NOTE: Contours in meters

Lens, Douai, Drocourt, Vimy, Arras, Queant

GROUP SOUCHEZ
XXIV
FIRST HORNE
CAN.
GROUP VIMY
SIXTH FALKENHAUSEN
XVII
GROUP ARRAS
THIRD ALLENBY
VI, XII

NOTE: Only Allied and German divisions on the front line are shown.

Morning 9 April
Evening 9 April
12 April
15 April

(6 miles)
(4 miles)

ARRAS AND VICINITY
BATTLE OF ARRAS
APRIL 1917

0 1 2 3
SCALE OF MILES

NORTHWEST EUROPE, 1914
WESTERN FRONT, 1917
General Situation January 1917;
German Withdrawal From Noyon Salient
and Nivelle's Final Plan of Attack

ELEVATIONS IN METERS
200 400 800 OVER

0 10 20 30 40
SCALE OF MILES

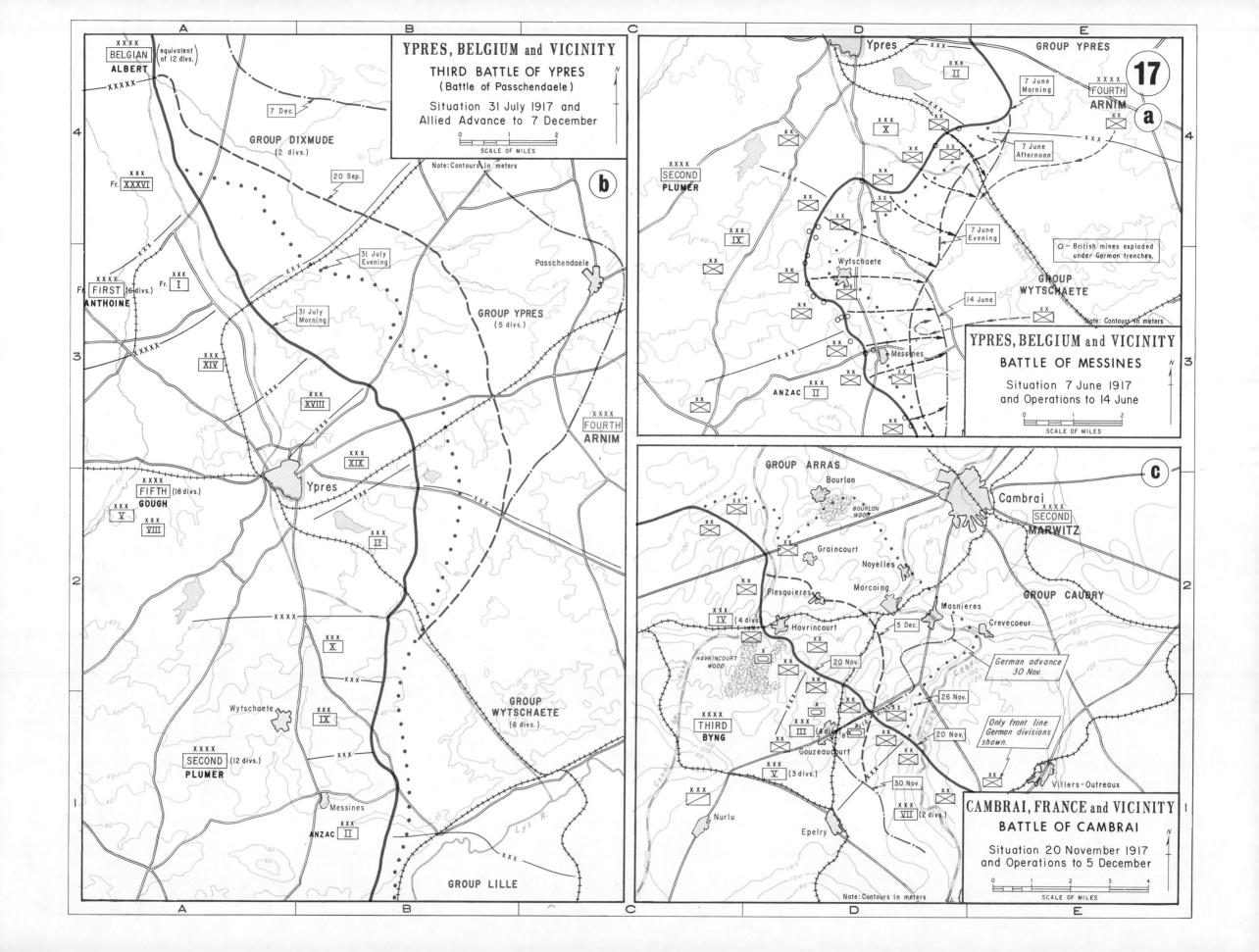

A **B** **C** **D** **E**

XXXX
BELGIAN
ALBERT (equivalent of 12 divs.)

XXXXX

7 Dec.

GROUP DIXMUDE
(2 divs.)

20 Sep.

XXX
Fr. XXXVI

31 July Evening

XXXX XXX
Fr. FIRST (6 divs.) Fr. I
ANTHOINE

Passchendaele

31 July Morning

GROUP YPRES
(5 divs.)

XXX
XIV

XXX
XVIII

XXX
XIX

Ypres

GROUP
WYTSCHAETE
(8 divs.)

XXXX
FOURTH
ARNIM

XXXX
FIFTH (18 divs.)
GOUGH

XXX
V

XXX
VIII

XXX
X

XXX
II

Wytschaete

XXX
IX

XXXX
SECOND (12 divs.)
PLUMER

Messines

ANZAC XXX
II

Lys R.

GROUP LILLE

YPRES, BELGIUM and VICINITY
THIRD BATTLE OF YPRES
(Battle of Passchendaele)
Situation 31 July 1917 and
Allied Advance to 7 December

0   1   2
SCALE OF MILES

Note: Contours in meters

b

Ypres XXX

GROUP YPRES

XXX
II

7 June
Morning

XXXX
FOURTH
ARNIM

XX

17

a

XXX
X

7 June
Afternoon

XXXX
SECOND
PLUMER

XX

XX

7 June
Evening

XXX
IX

Wytschaete

14 June

O – British mines exploded
under German trenches.

XX

GROUP
WYTSCHAETE

XX

XXX
ANZAC II

Messines

XX

XX

Note: Contours in meters

YPRES, BELGIUM and VICINITY
BATTLE OF MESSINES
Situation 7 June 1917
and Operations to 14 June

0   1   2
SCALE OF MILES

GROUP ARRAS

Bourlon

c

XX

BOURLON
WOOD

Cambrai

XXXX
SECOND
MARWITZ

XX

Graincourt

Noyelles

XX

Flesquieres

Marcoing

Masnieres

GROUP CAUBRY

XXX
IV (4 divs.)

Havrincourt

5 Dec.

Crevecoeur

HAVRINCOURT
WOOD

20 Nov.

German advance
30 Nov.

XXXX
THIRD
BYNG

XXX
III (4 divs.)

26 Nov.

Only front line
German divisions
shown.

20 Nov.

Gouzeaucourt

30 Nov.

XXX
V (3 divs.)

Villers-Outreaux

XXX
VII (2 divs.)

Nurlu

Epelry

CAMBRAI, FRANCE and VICINITY
BATTLE OF CAMBRAI
Situation 20 November 1917
and Operations to 5 December

Note: Contours in meters

0   1   2   3   4
SCALE OF MILES

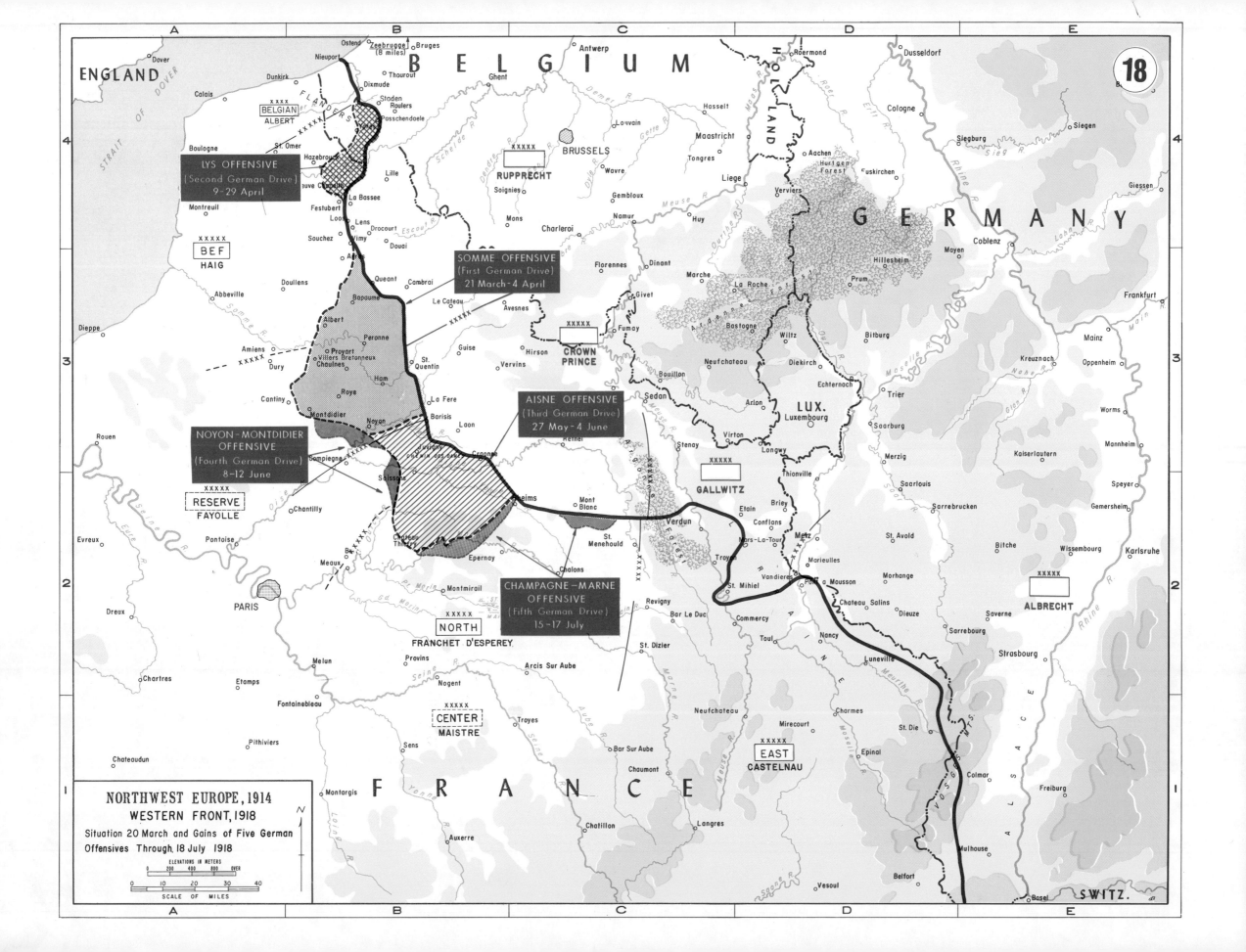

ENGLAND

BELGIUM

GERMANY

HOLLAND

LUX.

FRANCE

SWITZ.

LYS OFFENSIVE
(Second German Drive)
9-29 April

xxxx
BELGIAN
ALBERT

xxxxx
BEF
HAIG

xxxxx
RUPPRECHT

xxxxx
BRUSSELS

SOMME OFFENSIVE
(First German Drive)
21 March-4 April

xxxxx
CROWN
PRINCE

AISNE OFFENSIVE
(Third German Drive)
27 May-4 June

**NOYON-MONTDIDIER
OFFENSIVE**
(Fourth German Drive)
8-12 June

xxxxx
RESERVE
FAYOLLE

xxxxx
GALLWITZ

xxxxx
ALBRECHT

**CHAMPAGNE-MARNE
OFFENSIVE**
(Fifth German Drive)
15-17 July

xxxxx
NORTH
FRANCHET D'ESPEREY

xxxxx
CENTER
MAISTRE

xxxxx
EAST
CASTELNAU

NORTHWEST EUROPE, 1914
WESTERN FRONT, 1918

Situation 20 March and Gains of Five German
Offensives Through 18 July 1918

ELEVATIONS IN METERS
0 200 400 800 OVER

0 10 20 30 40
SCALE OF MILES

18

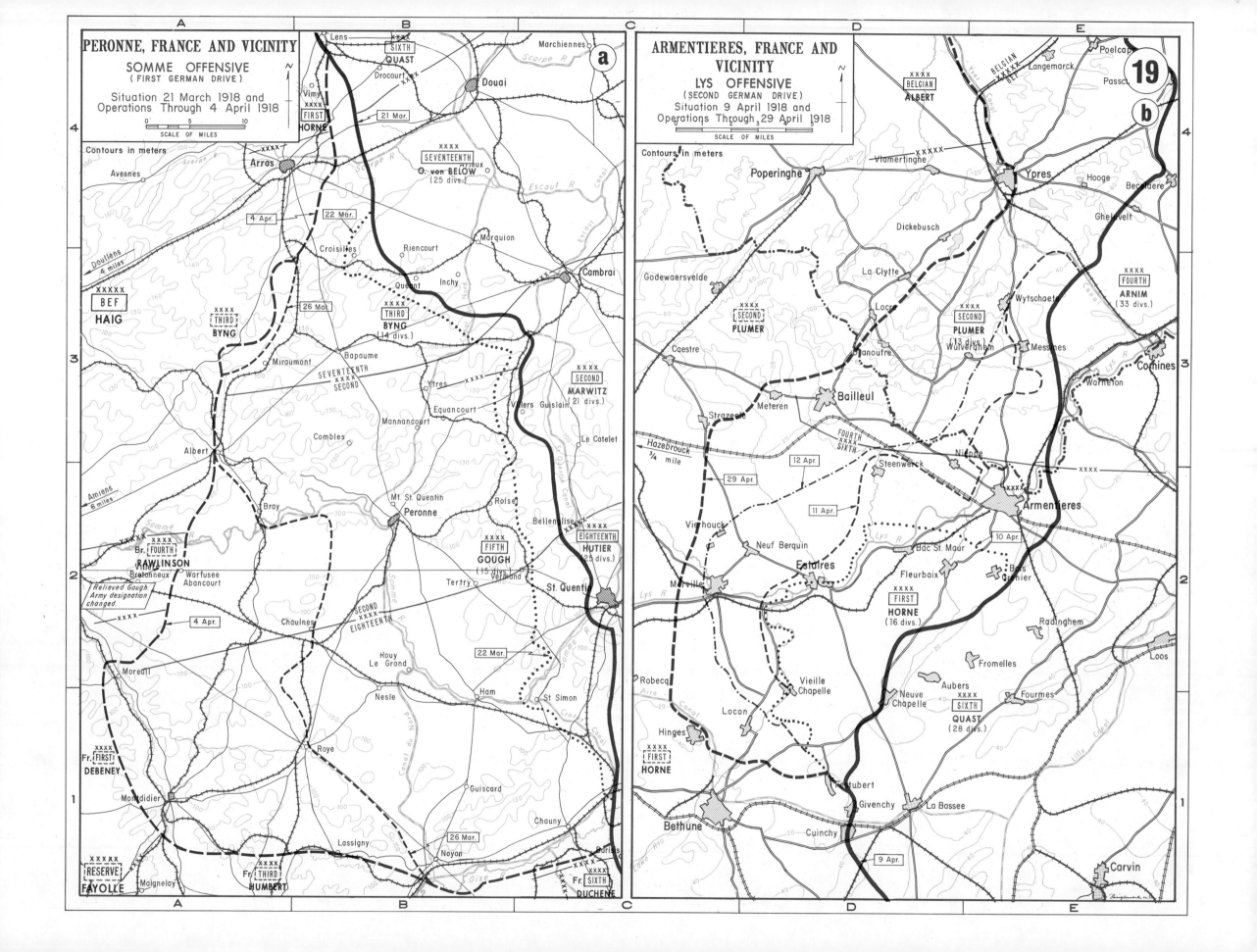

PERONNE, FRANCE AND VICINITY

SOMME OFFENSIVE
(FIRST GERMAN DRIVE)

Situation 21 March 1918 and
Operations Through 4 April 1918

SCALE OF MILES

Contours in meters

ARMENTIERES, FRANCE AND VICINITY

LYS OFFENSIVE
(SECOND GERMAN DRIVE)

Situation 9 April 1918 and
Operations Through 29 April 1918

SCALE OF MILES

Contours in meters

19
a
b

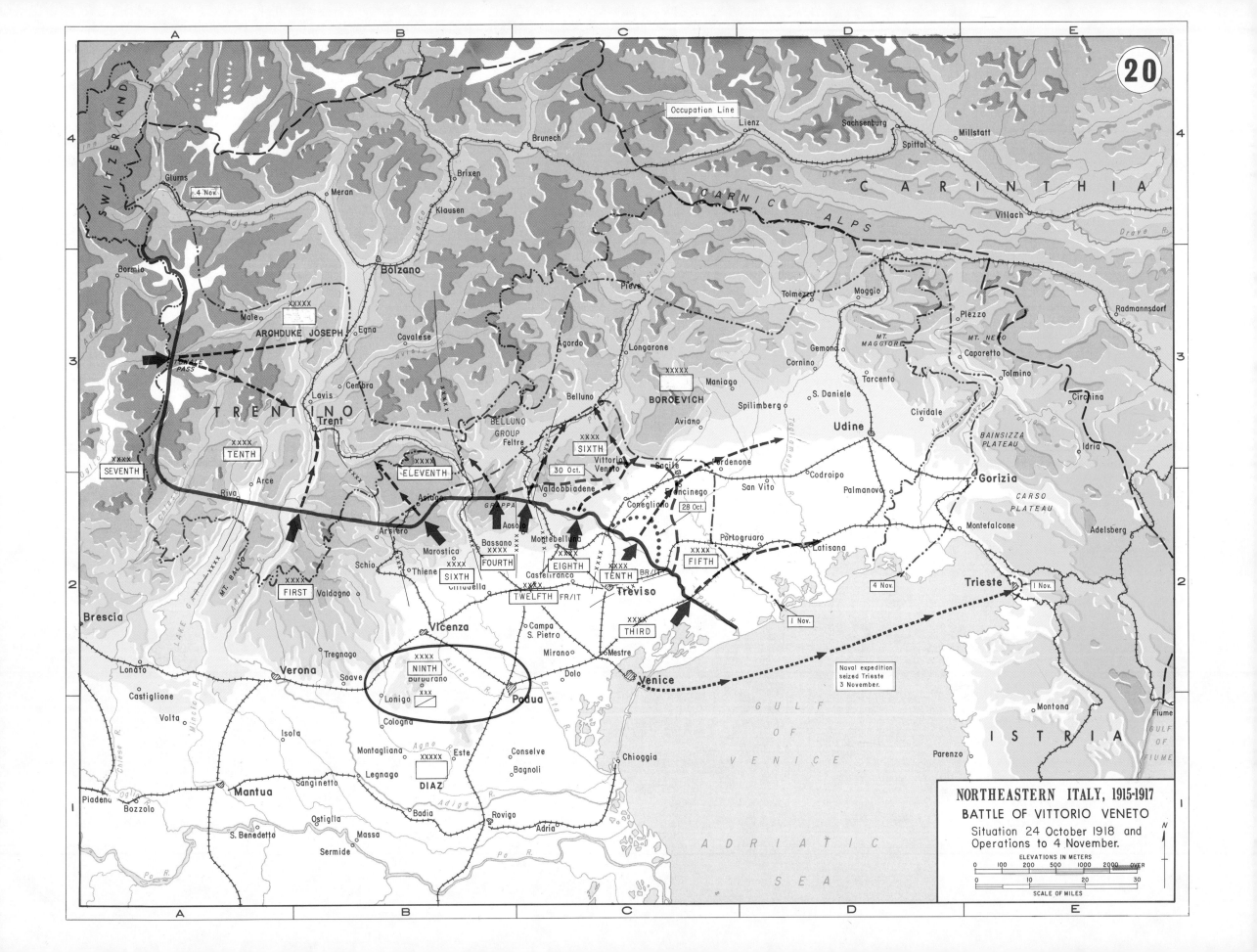

NORTHEASTERN ITALY, 1915-1917
BATTLE OF VITTORIO VENETO
Situation 24 October 1918 and
Operations to 4 November.

ELEVATIONS IN METERS
0 100 200 500 1000 2000 OVER

0   10   20   30
SCALE OF MILES

Naval expedition
seized Trieste
3 November.

Occupation Line

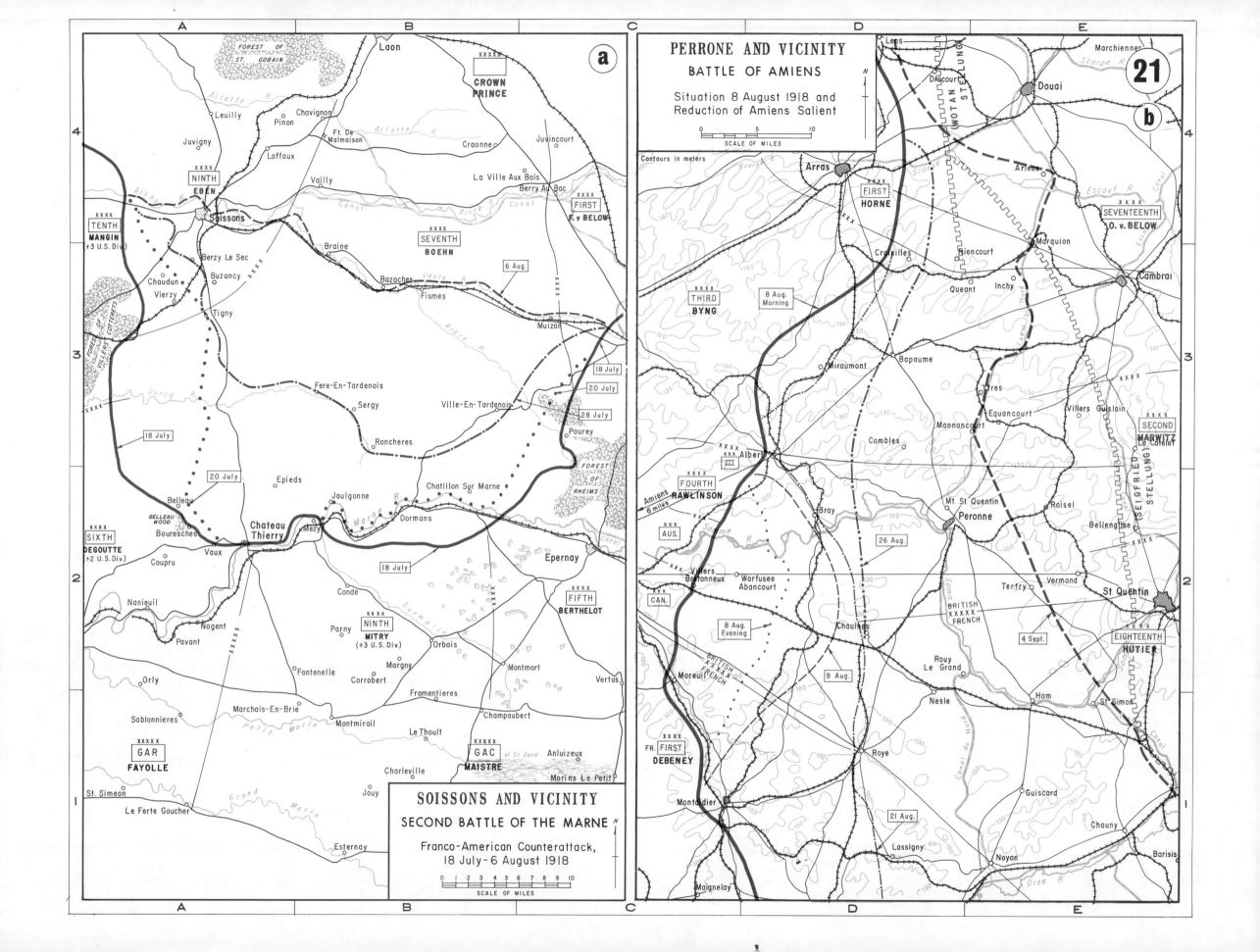

a

FOREST OF ST. GOBAIN

Laon

XXXX
CROWN PRINCE

Leuilly
Pinon
Chavignon
Ft. De Malmaison
Craonne
Juvincourt

Juvigny
Laffaux
Vailly
La Ville Aux Bois
Berry Au Bac

XXXX
NINTH
EBEN

Soissons

XXXX
FIRST
F. v BELOW

XXXX
TENTH
MANGIN
(+3 U.S. Div.)

Berzy Le Sec
Braine

XXXX
SEVENTH
BOEHN

Buzancy
Bazoches
Vesle R.
Muizon

Chaudun
Vierzy
Fismes

Tigny

6 Aug.

FORETS DE VILLERS COTERETS

Fere-En-Tardenois

18 July

Sergy
Ville-En-Tardenois

20 July

Ourcq R.

Roncheres

Pourcy
28 July

18 July

Epieds

FOREST OF RHEIMS

20 July

Belleau
Chatillon Sur Marne

BELLEAU WOOD
Boursches
Jaulgonne
Dormans

XXXX
SIXTH
DEGOUTTE
(+2 U.S. Div.)

Chateau Thierry
Mezy
Vaux

Marne R.

Epernay

Coupru

Nanieuil

Conde

18 July

XXXX
FIFTH
BERTHELOT

Nogent
Parny

XXXX
NINTH
MITRY
(+3 U.S. Div.)

Orbais

Pavant

Fontenelle
Margny
Montmort
Vertus

Orly
Corrobert

XXXXX
GAR
FAYOLLE

Marchais-En-Brie
Fromentieres

XXXXX
GAC
MAISTRE

Sablonnieres
Montmirail
Le Thoult
Champaubert
Anluizeux

St. Simeon
Le Ferte Gaucher
Petit Morin
Jouy
Morins Le Petit

Grand Morin
Esternay

Barisis

SOISSONS AND VICINITY

SECOND BATTLE OF THE MARNE

Franco-American Counterattack,
18 July–6 August 1918

0 1 2 3 4 5 6 7 8 9 10
SCALE OF MILES

b

PERRONE AND VICINITY

BATTLE OF AMIENS

Situation 8 August 1918 and
Reduction of Amiens Salient

0   5   10
SCALE OF MILES

Contours in meters

21

Lens
Marchiennes
Scarpe R.
Dracourt

WOTAN STELLUNG

Douai

Arras

XXX

XXXX
FIRST
HORNE

Arleux

XXXX
SEVENTEENTH
O. v. BELOW

XXXX
THIRD
BYNG

8 Aug.
Morning

Croisilles
Riencourt
Marquion

Queant
Inchy
Cambrai

Miraumont
Bapaume

Ytres
130
Villers Guislain

Equancourt

XXXX
SECOND
MARWITZ

XXXX
Albert
III
Combles
Mannancourt
Le Catelet

XXX
FOURTH
RAWLINSON

Bray
Mt. St. Quentin
Roisel

SIEGFRIED STELLUNG

XXX
AUS.

Amiens
6 miles

Somme R.

26 Aug.
Peronne
Bellenglise

Villers Bretonneux
Warfusee Abancourt

XXX
CAN.

Tertry
Vermand
St. Quentin

8 Aug.
Evening

Chaulnes

BRITISH
XXXXX
FRENCH

Moreuil

9 Aug.

Rouy Le Grand

4 Sept.

XXXX
EIGHTEENTH
HUTIER

BRITISH
XXXXX
FRENCH

Nesle

Ham
St. Simon

FR. FIRST
DEBENEY

Montdidier

Roye

21 Aug.

Guiscard

Chauny

Maignelay
Lassigny
Noyon

Oise R.

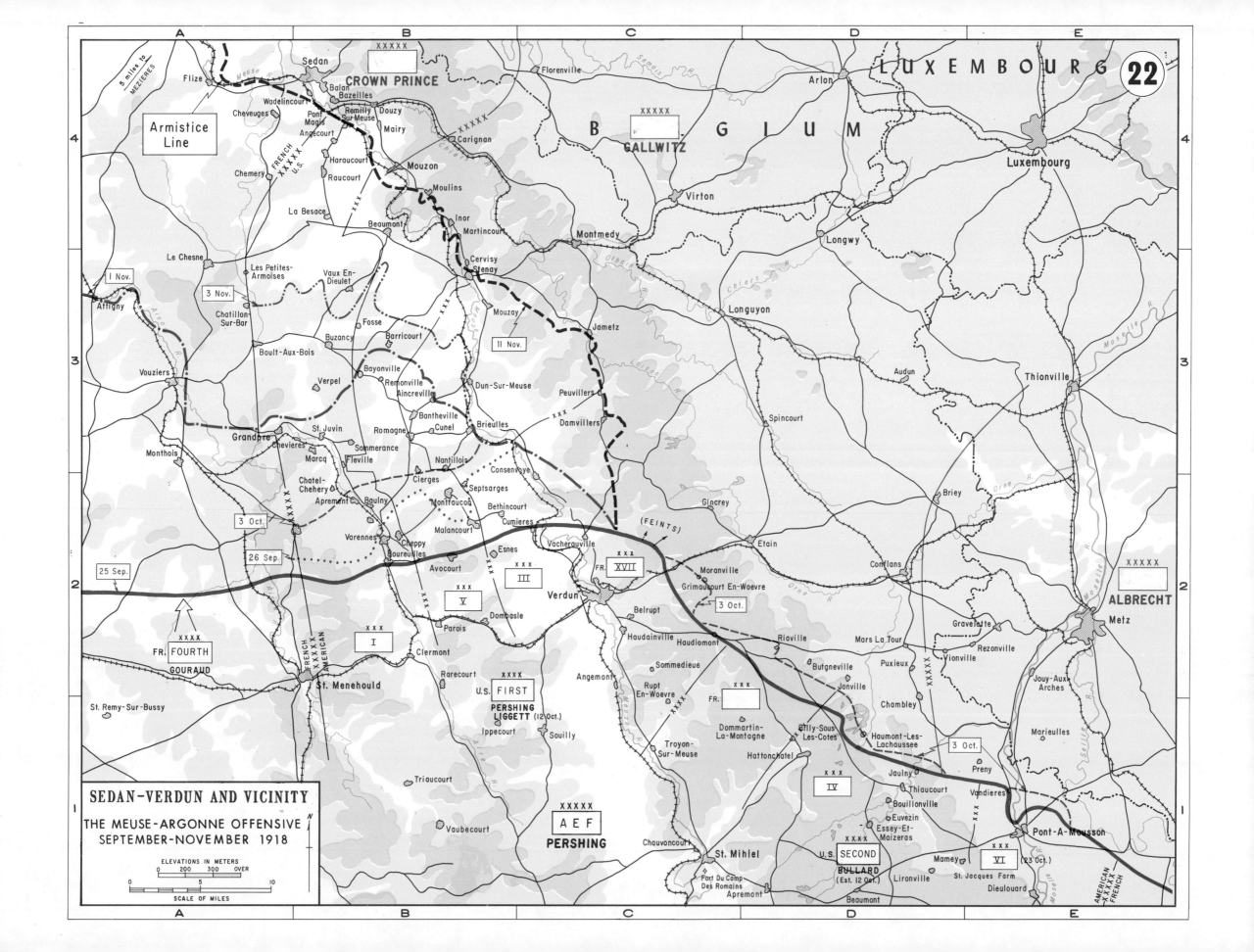

SEDAN-VERDUN AND VICINITY

THE MEUSE-ARGONNE OFFENSIVE
SEPTEMBER-NOVEMBER 1918

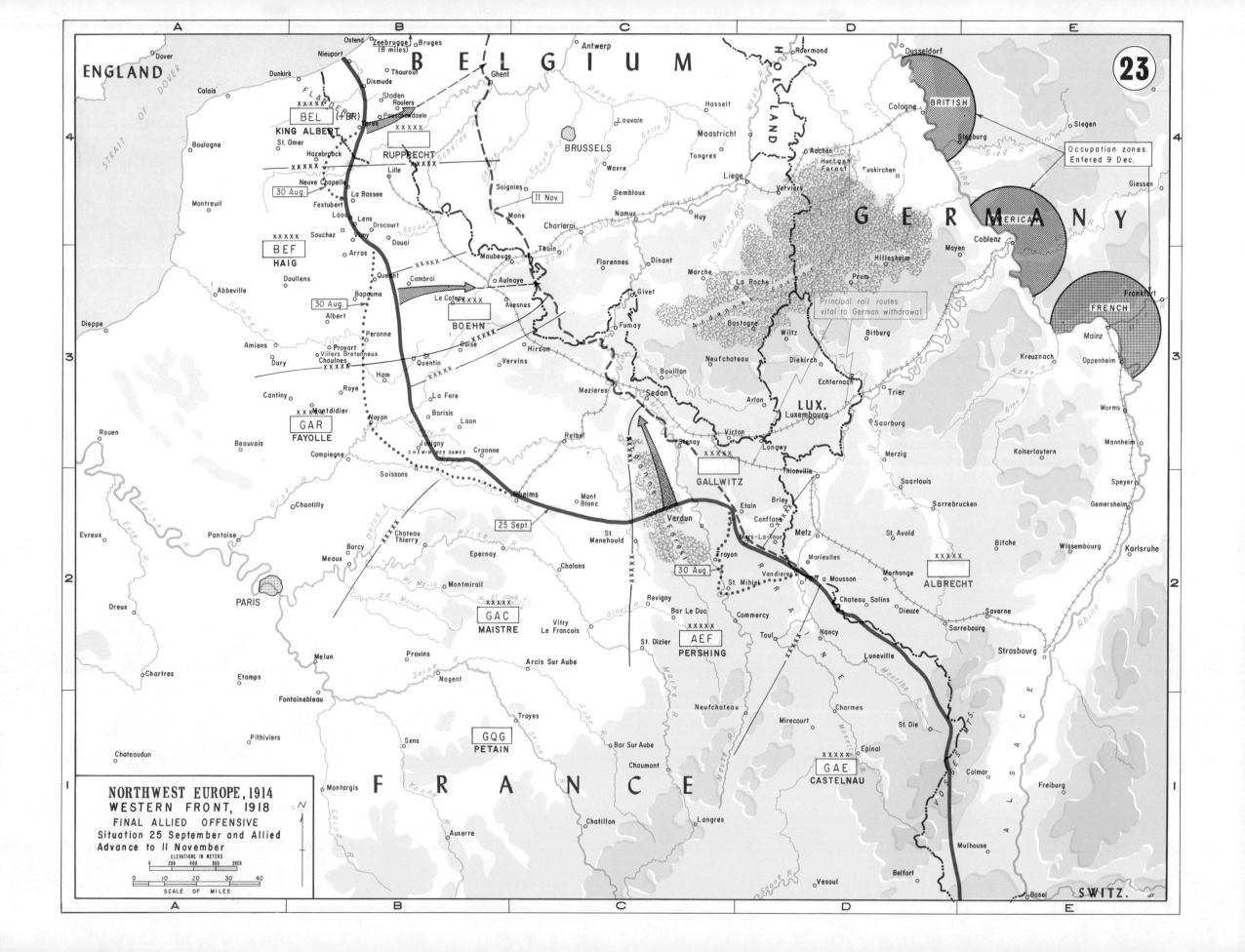

NORTHWEST EUROPE, 1914
WESTERN FRONT, 1918
FINAL ALLIED OFFENSIVE
Situation 25 September and Allied
Advance to 11 November

ELEVATIONS IN METERS
0   200   400   600   800   OVER

0   10   20   30   40
SCALE OF MILES

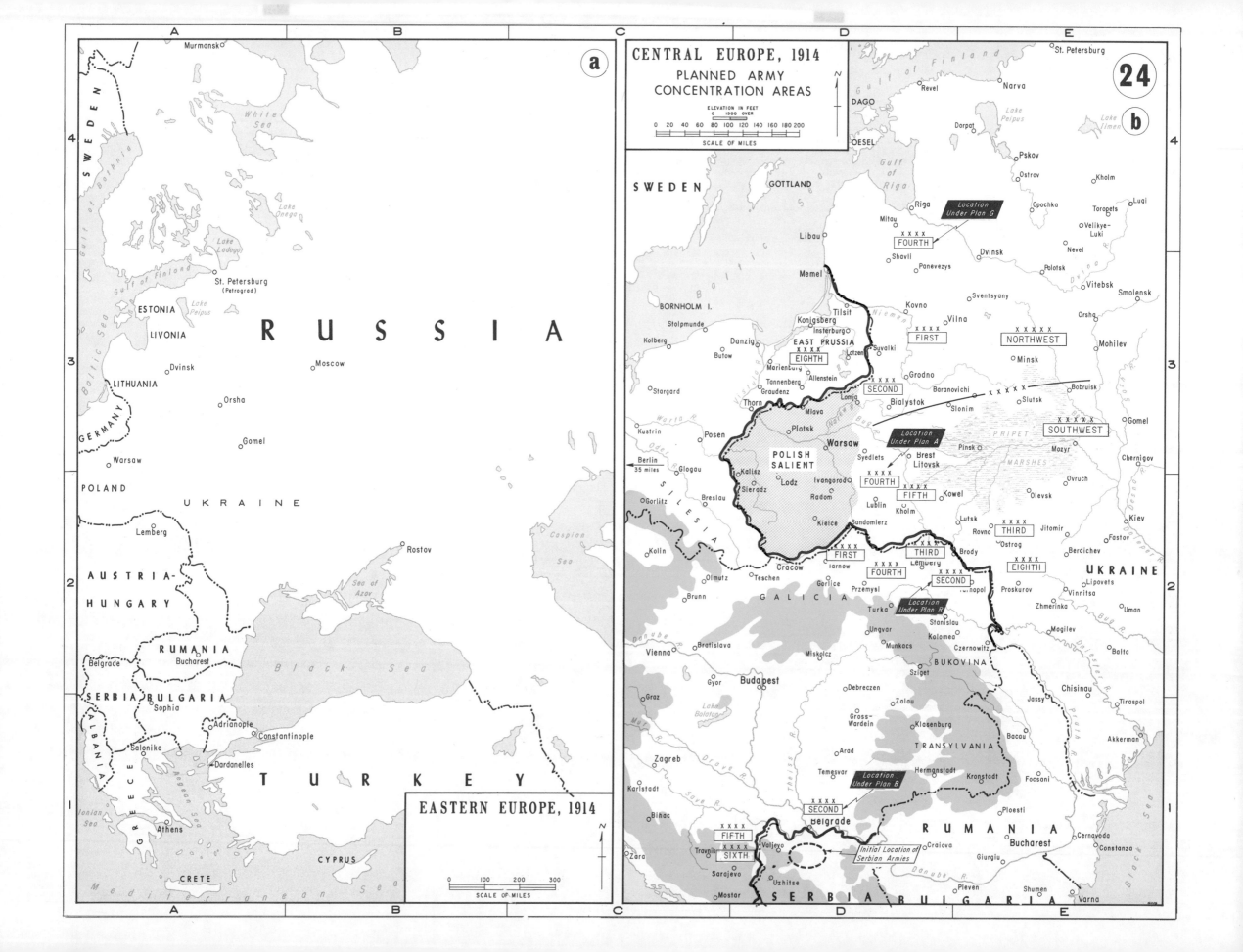

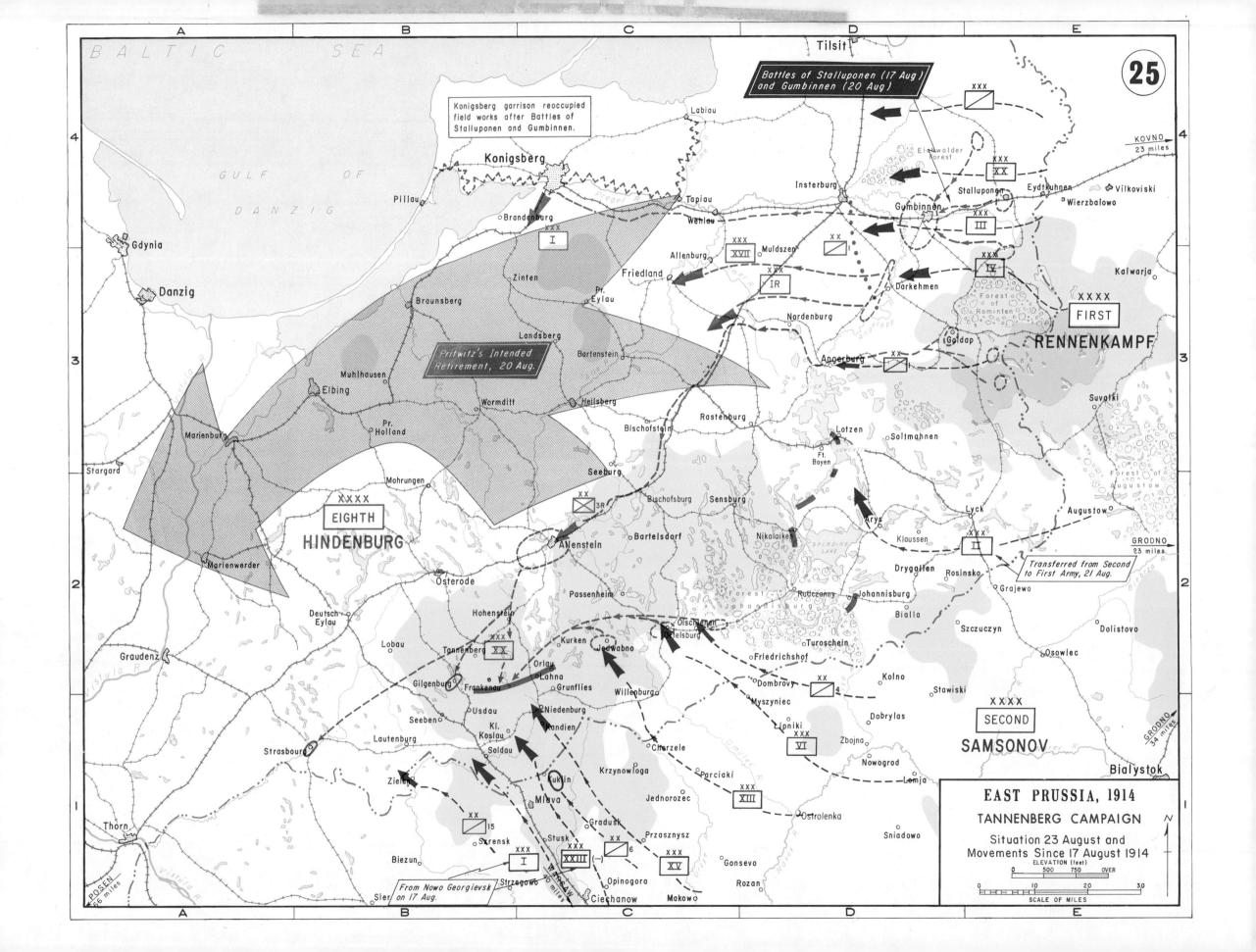

BALTIC SEA

Tilsit

Battles of Stalluponen (17 Aug) and Gumbinnen (20 Aug)

KOVNO
23 miles

Konigsberg garrison reoccupied field works after Battles of Stalluponen and Gumbinnen.

Labiau

GULF OF DANZIG

Konigsberg

Pillau

Brandenburg

I

Insterburg

Stalluponen

Eydtkuhnen

Vilkoviski
Wierzbalowo

XXX
XX

Tapiau
Wehlau

Gumbinnen

III

Allenburg
Muldszen
Darkehmen

XX

IV

Kalwarja

Gdynia

Danzig

Zinten

Friedland

XVII

XXX
IR

XXX

FIRST

RENNENKAMPF

Braunsberg
Pr. Eylau

Nordenburg

Stargard

Landsberg

Bartenstein

Angerburg

XX

Suvalki

Pritwitz's Intended Retirement, 20 Aug.

Muhlhausen

Elbing

Wormditt

Heilsberg

Rastenburg

Lotzen
Ft. Boyen

Soltmahnen

Marienburg

Pr. Holland

Bischofstein

Goldap

Arys

Lyck

Augustow

Mohrungen

Seeburg

Bischofsburg
Sensburg

Nikolaiken

Klaussen

II

GRODNO
23 miles

XXXX
EIGHTH
HINDENBURG

Osterode

XX
3R

Allenstein
Bartelsdorf

SPIRDING LAKE

Drygallen
Rosinsko

Grajewo

Transferred from Second to First Army, 21 Aug.

Marienwerder

Deutsch Eylau

Passenheim

Johannisburg

Bialla

Szczuczyn

Dolistovo

Graudenz

Lobau

Hohenstein

Kurken
Jedwabno

Orteisburg
Olschanen

Turoschein

Rudczanny

Friedrichsdorf

Kolno

Stawiski

Osowiec

Tannenberg

XXX
XX

Orlau
Lahna
Grunflies

Willenburg

Dombrovy

XX
4

Stargard

Gilgenburg
Frankenau

Niedenburg

Myszyniec

Zbojna

Dobrylas

XXXX
SECOND

SAMSONOV

Lautenburg

Usdau

Kl. Koslau
Soldau
Kandien

Charzele

Lipniki

XXX
VI

Nowogrod

Lomja

Bialystok

Strasbourg

Zielun

Mlava

Gradusk
Krzynowloga

Parciaki

Jednorozec

Ostrolenka

GRODNO
34 miles

Thorn

Kuklin

Stusk
Przasnysz

XXX
XIII

Gonsevo

Sniadowo

EAST PRUSSIA, 1914

Biezun
Sxrensk

XX
15

XXX
I

XXX
XXIII (−)

XX
6

XXX
XV

Opinogora

Makowo

Rozan

TANNENBERG CAMPAIGN

Situation 23 August and Movements Since 17 August 1914

POSEN
66 miles

Sier

From Nowo Georgievsk on 17 Aug.

Strzegowo

Ciechanow

WARSAW
70 miles

ELEVATION (feet)

| 0 | 500 | 750 | OVER |

0 10 20 30
SCALE OF MILES

25

N

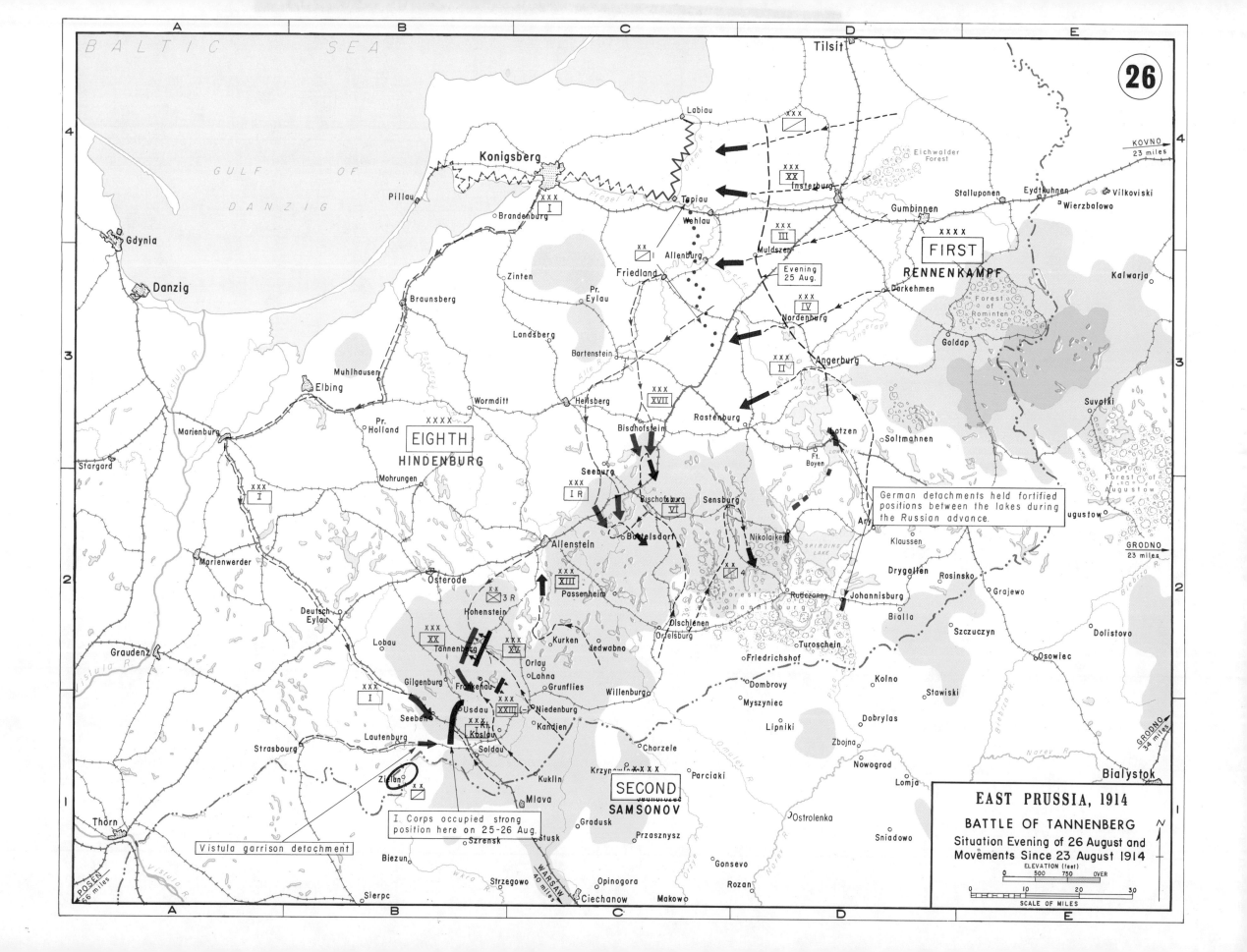

BATTLE OF TANNENBERG

Situation Evening of 26 August and
Movements Since 23 August 1914

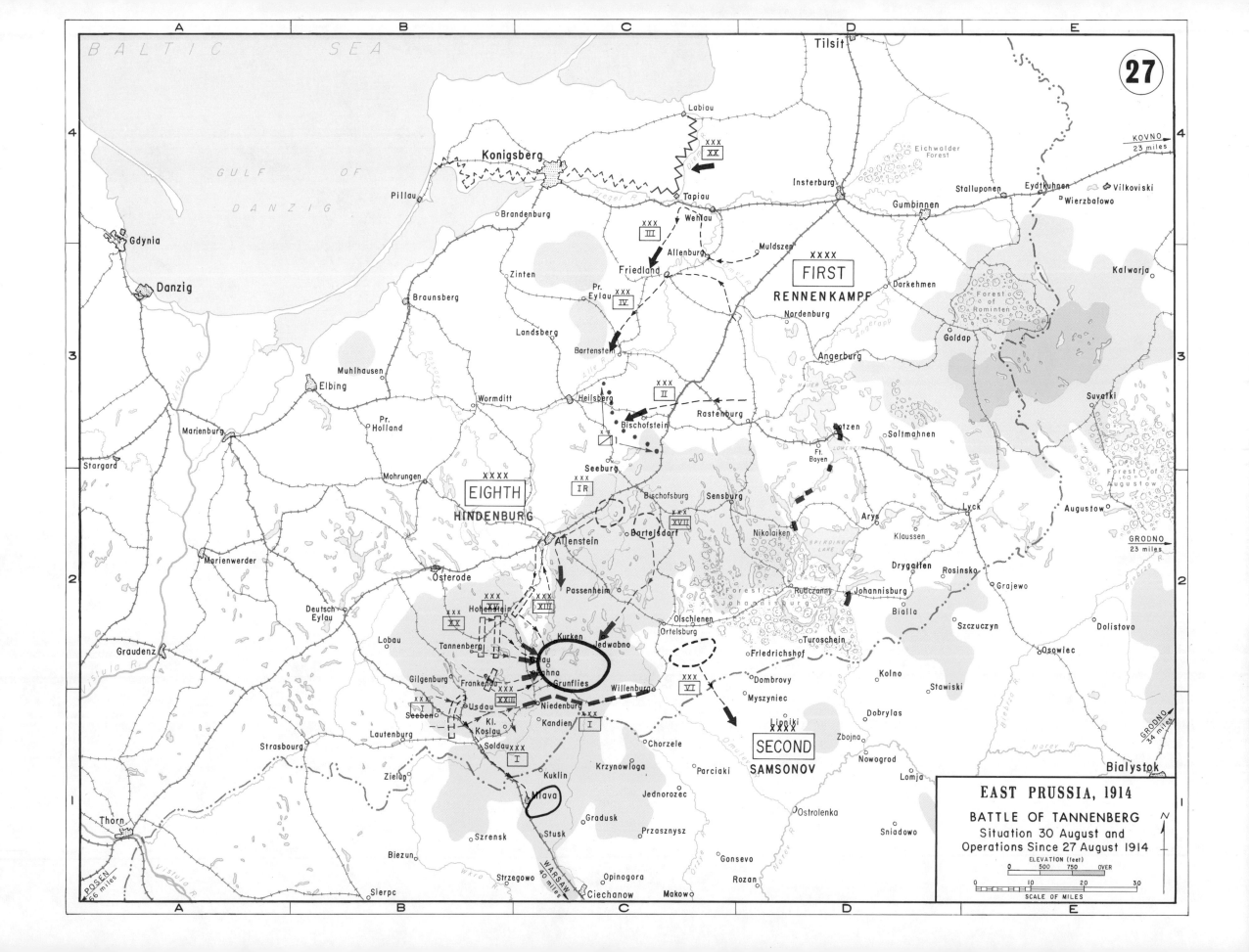

EAST PRUSSIA, 1914

BATTLE OF TANNENBERG

Situation 30 August and
Operations Since 27 August 1914

ELEVATION (feet)

500 750 OVER

0 10 20 30

SCALE OF MILES

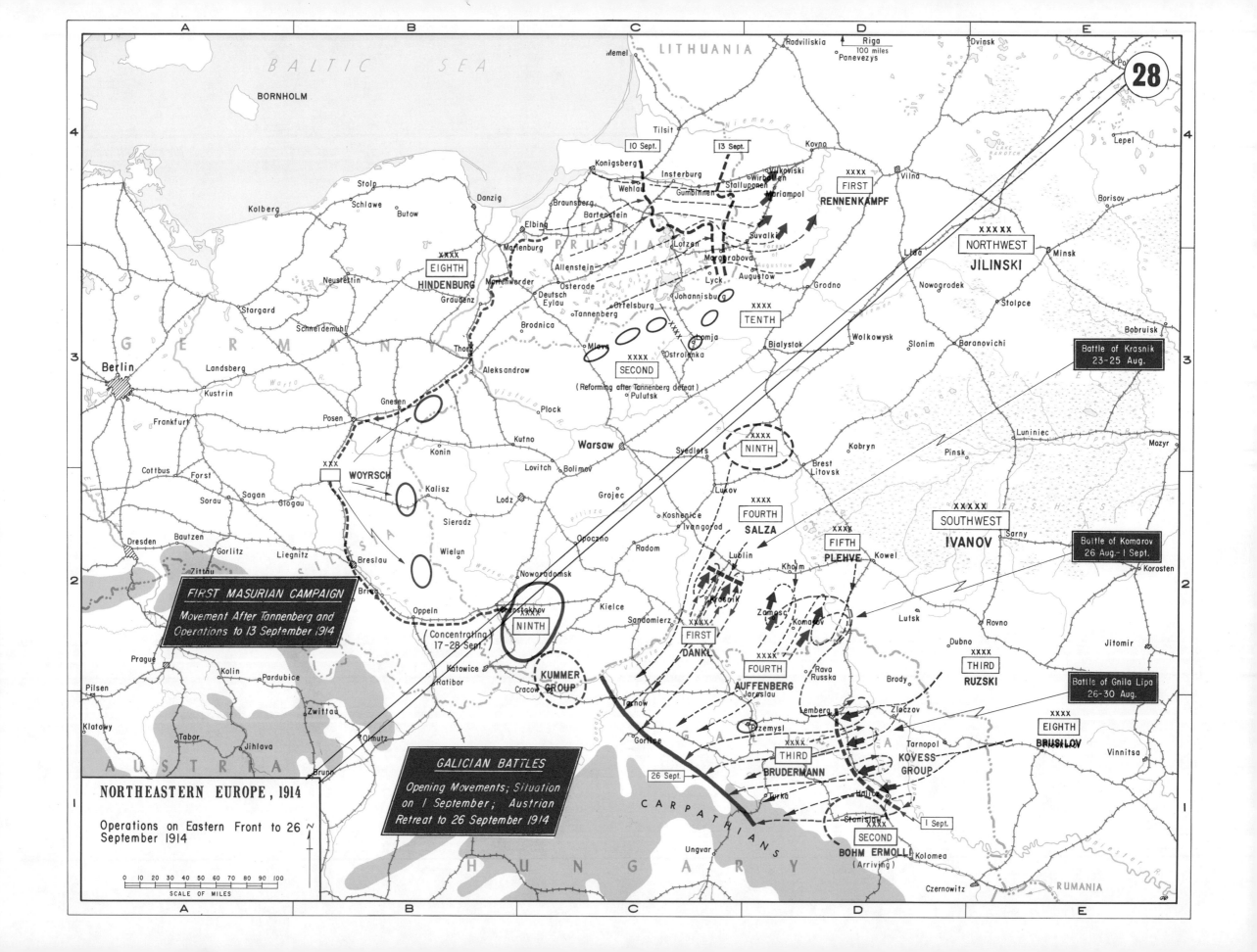

NORTHEASTERN EUROPE, 1914

Operations on Eastern Front to 26 September 1914

FIRST MASURIAN CAMPAIGN

Movement After Tannenberg and Operations to 13 September 1914

GALICIAN BATTLES

Opening Movements; Situation on 1 September; Austrian Retreat to 26 September 1914

Battle of Krasnik 23-25 Aug.

Battle of Komarov 26 Aug.- 1 Sept.

Battle of Gnila Lipa 26-30 Aug.

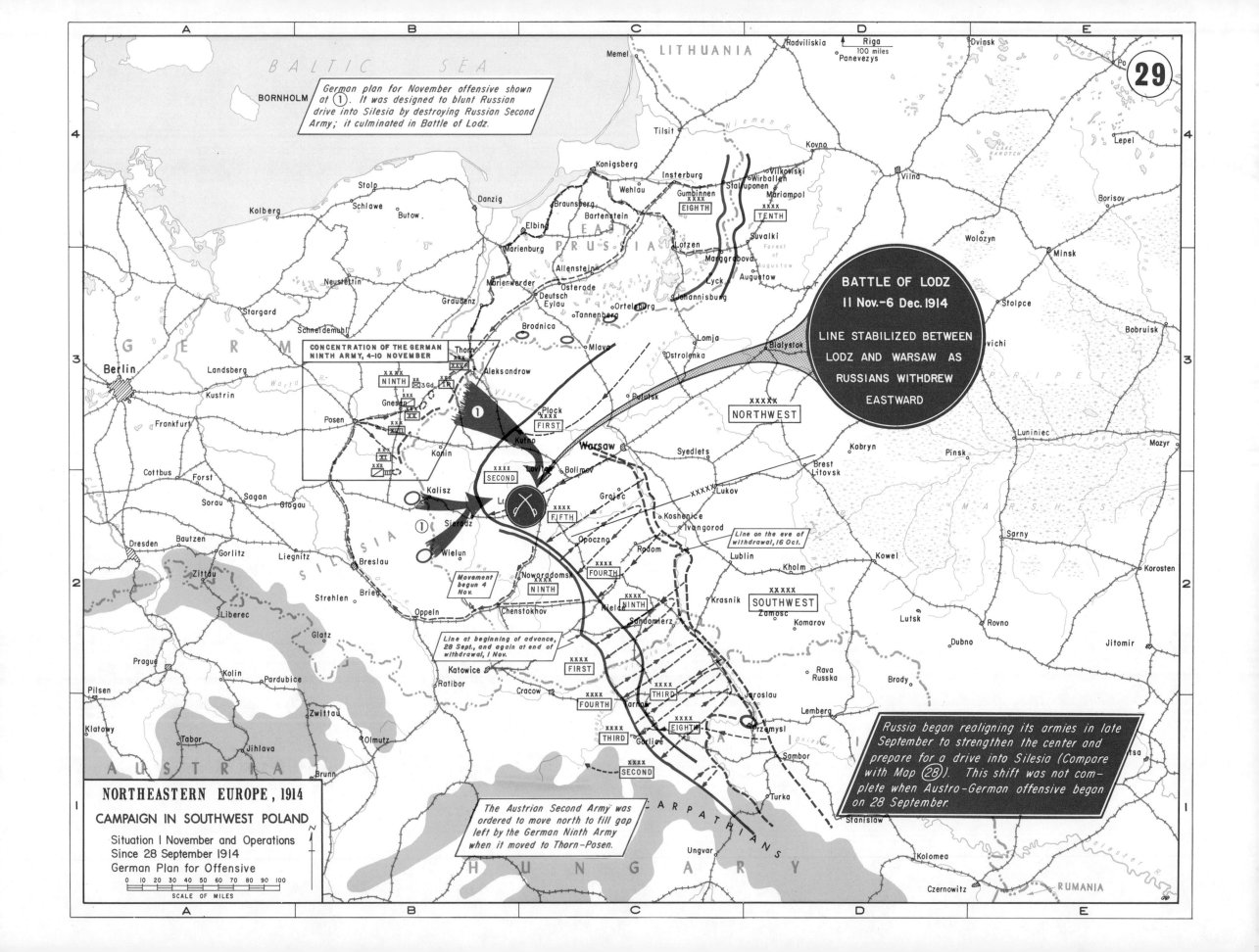

29

BALTIC SEA

BORNHOLM

German plan for November offensive shown at ① . It was designed to blunt Russian drive into Silesia by destroying Russian Second Army; it culminated in Battle of Lodz.

LITHUANIA

Riga
100 miles

BATTLE OF LODZ
11 Nov.–6 Dec. 1914

LINE STABILIZED BETWEEN LODZ AND WARSAW AS RUSSIANS WITHDREW EASTWARD

CONCENTRATION OF THE GERMAN NINTH ARMY, 4-10 NOVEMBER

NINTH

NORTHWEST

FIRST

Movement begun 4 Nov.

SECOND

FIFTH

Line on the eve of withdrawal, 16 Oct.

FOURTH

NINTH

SOUTHWEST

Line at beginning of advance, 28 Sept., and again at end of withdrawal, 1 Nov.

FIRST

NINTH

THIRD

Russia began realigning its armies in late September to strengthen the center and prepare for a drive into Silesia (Compare with Map ㉘). This shift was not complete when Austro-German offensive began on 28 September.

FOURTH

EIGHTH

THIRD

SECOND

CARPATHIANS

The Austrian Second Army was ordered to move north to fill gap left by the German Ninth Army when it moved to Thorn-Posen.

HUNGARY

RUMANIA

NORTHEASTERN EUROPE, 1914

CAMPAIGN IN SOUTHWEST POLAND

Situation 1 November and Operations Since 28 September 1914
German Plan for Offensive

0 10 20 30 40 50 60 70 80 90 100
SCALE OF MILES

BALTIC SEA

BORNHOLM

LITHUANIA

30

NORTHEASTERN EUROPE, 1914

WINTER BATTLE OF MASURIA

Situation 7 February and Operations
to 18 February 1915

SCALE OF MILES
0 10 20 30 40 50 60 70 80 90 100

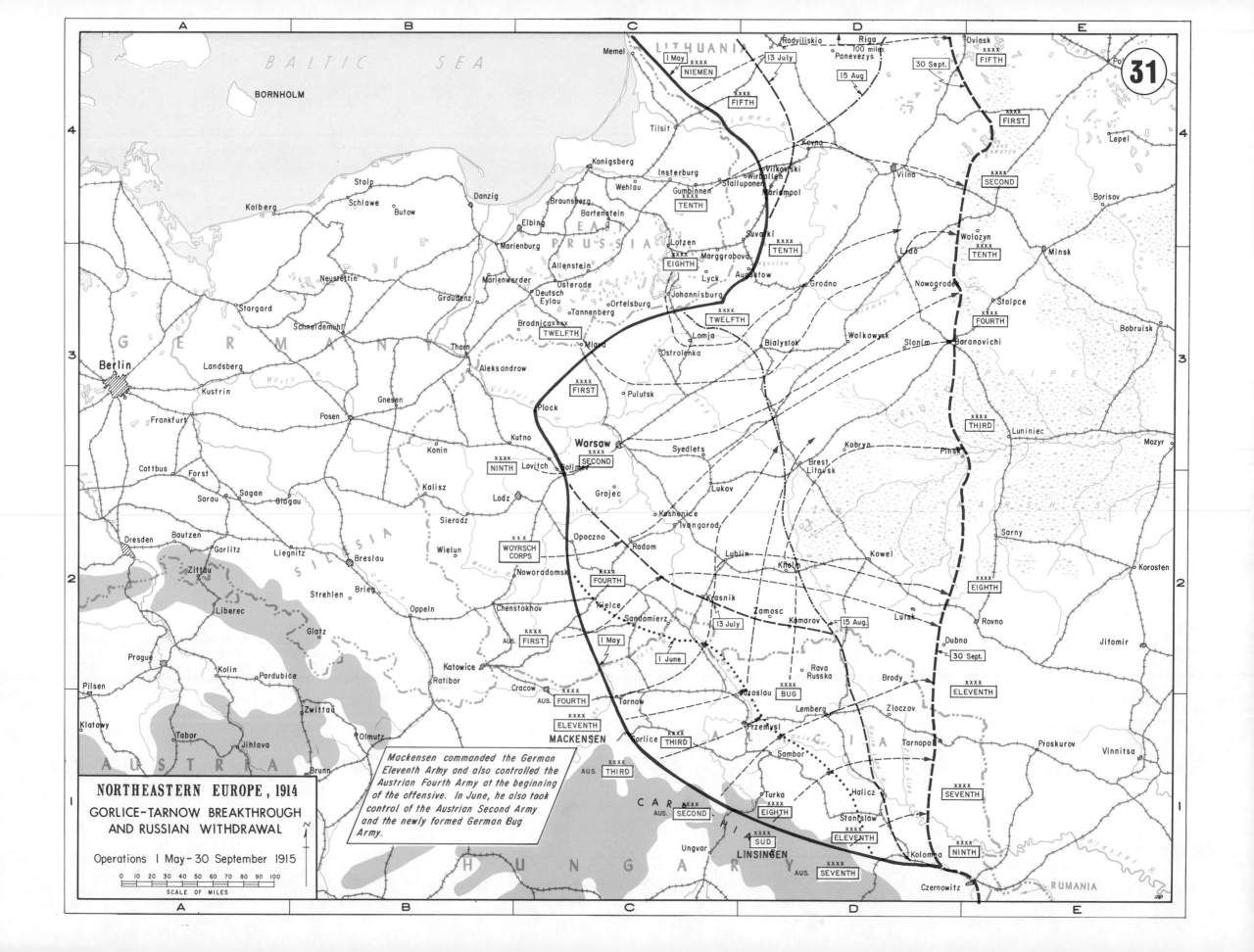

NORTHEASTERN EUROPE, 1914

GORLICE-TARNOW BREAKTHROUGH
AND RUSSIAN WITHDRAWAL

Operations 1 May-30 September 1915

0 10 20 30 40 50 60 70 80 90 100
SCALE OF MILES

Mackensen commanded the German Eleventh Army and also controlled the Austrian Fourth Army at the beginning of the offensive. In June, he also took control of the Austrian Second Army and the newly formed German Bug Army.

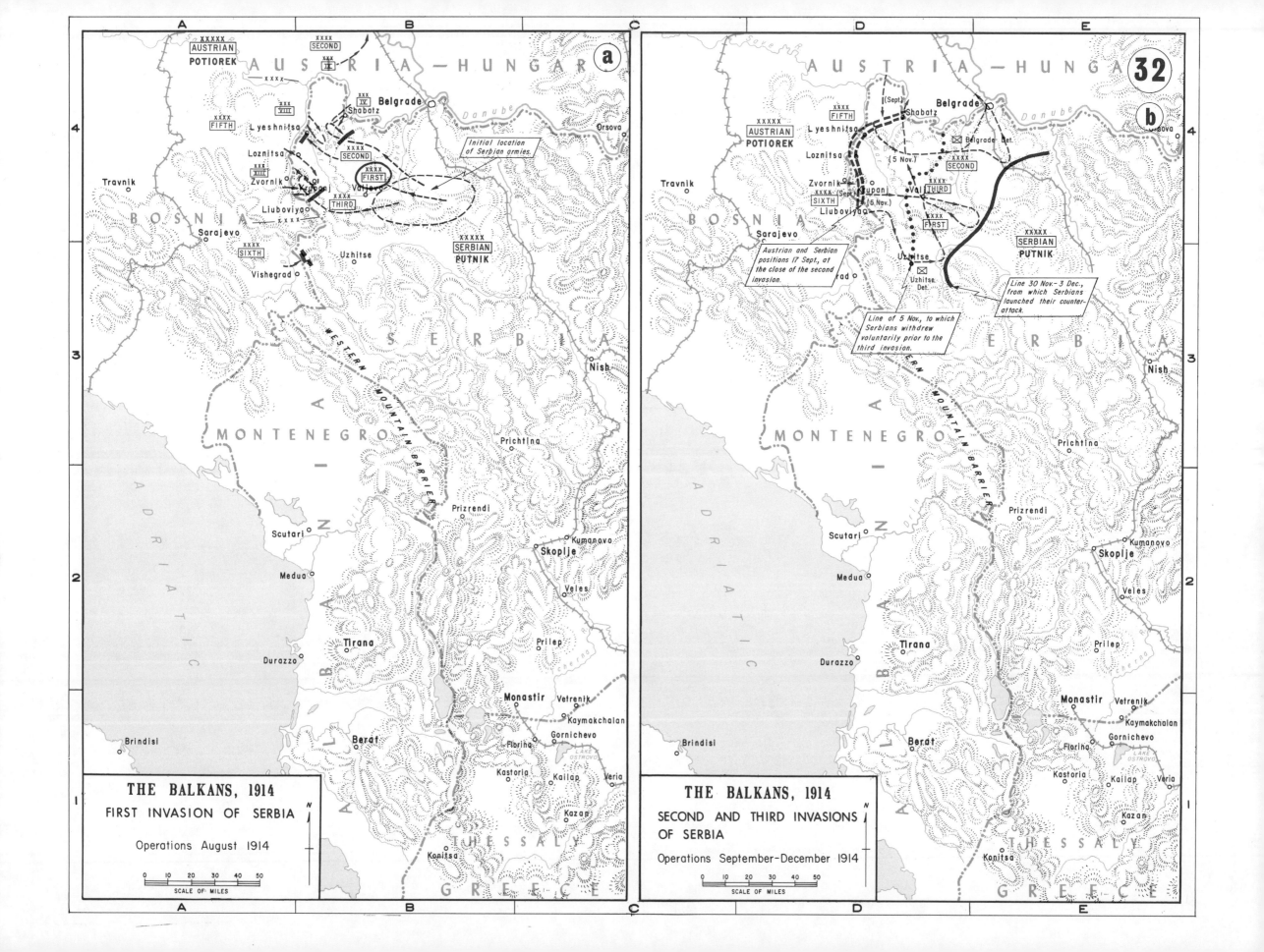

a

XXXX
AUSTRIAN
POTIOREK

XXXX
SECOND

AUSTRIA — HUNGARY

Belgrade

Danube

Orsova

XXX
III

XXX
IV
Shabatz

XXXX
FIFTH

Lyeshnitsa

XXX
VIII

Loznitsa

XXXX
SECOND

XXX
XIII

Travnik

Zvornik

XXXX
FIRST

Krupanj

Valjevo

Initial location of Serbian armies.

Liuboviya

XXXX
THIRD

BOSNIA

Sarajevo

XXXX
SIXTH

Uzhitse

XXXXX
SERBIAN
PUTNIK

Vishegrad

WESTERN MOUNTAIN BARRIER

S E R B I A

Nish

M O N T E N E G R O

Prichtina

Drin

Prizrendi

A L B A N I A

Scutari

Kumanovo

Tcherna R.

Medua

Skoplje

Veles

Prilep

Tirana

Durazzo

Monastir

Vetrenik

Kaymakchalan

Gornichevo

Florina

LAKE OSTROVO

Brindisi

Berat

Kastoria

Kailap

Veria

Konitsa

Kazan

THESSALY

GREECE

THE BALKANS, 1914

FIRST INVASION OF SERBIA

Operations August 1914

N

0 10 20 30 40 50
SCALE OF MILES

b

32

AUSTRIA — HUNGARY

(Sept)

Belgrade

Sever... ?

Shabatz

Danube

Orsova

XXXXX
AUSTRIAN
POTIOREK

Lyeshnitsa

Belgrade Det.

Loznitsa

(5 Nov.)

XXXX
SECOND

Travnik

Zvornik

(Sept)

XXXX
SIXTH

Krupanj
(5 Nov.)

Val

XXXX
THIRD

Liuboviya

XXXX
FIRST

BOSNIA

Sarajevo

...grad

Uzhitse

Austrian and Serbian positions 17 Sept., at the close of the second invasion.

Uzhitse Det.

XXXXX
SERBIAN
PUTNIK

Line of 5 Nov., to which Serbians withdrew voluntarily prior to the third invasion.

Line 30 Nov.– 3 Dec., from which Serbians launched their counter-attack.

S E R B I A

Nish

M O N T E N E G R O

WESTERN MOUNTAIN BARRIER

Prichtina

Prizrendi

A L B A N I A

Scutari

Kumanovo

Tcherna R.

Medua

Skoplje

Veles

Prilep

Tirana

Durazzo

Monastir

Vetrenik

Kaymakchalan

Gornichevo

Florina

LAKE OSTROVO

Brindisi

Berat

Kastoria

Kailap

Veria

Konitsa

Kazan

THESSALY

GREECE

THE BALKANS, 1914

SECOND AND THIRD INVASIONS OF SERBIA

Operations September–December 1914

N

0 10 20 30 40 50
SCALE OF MILES

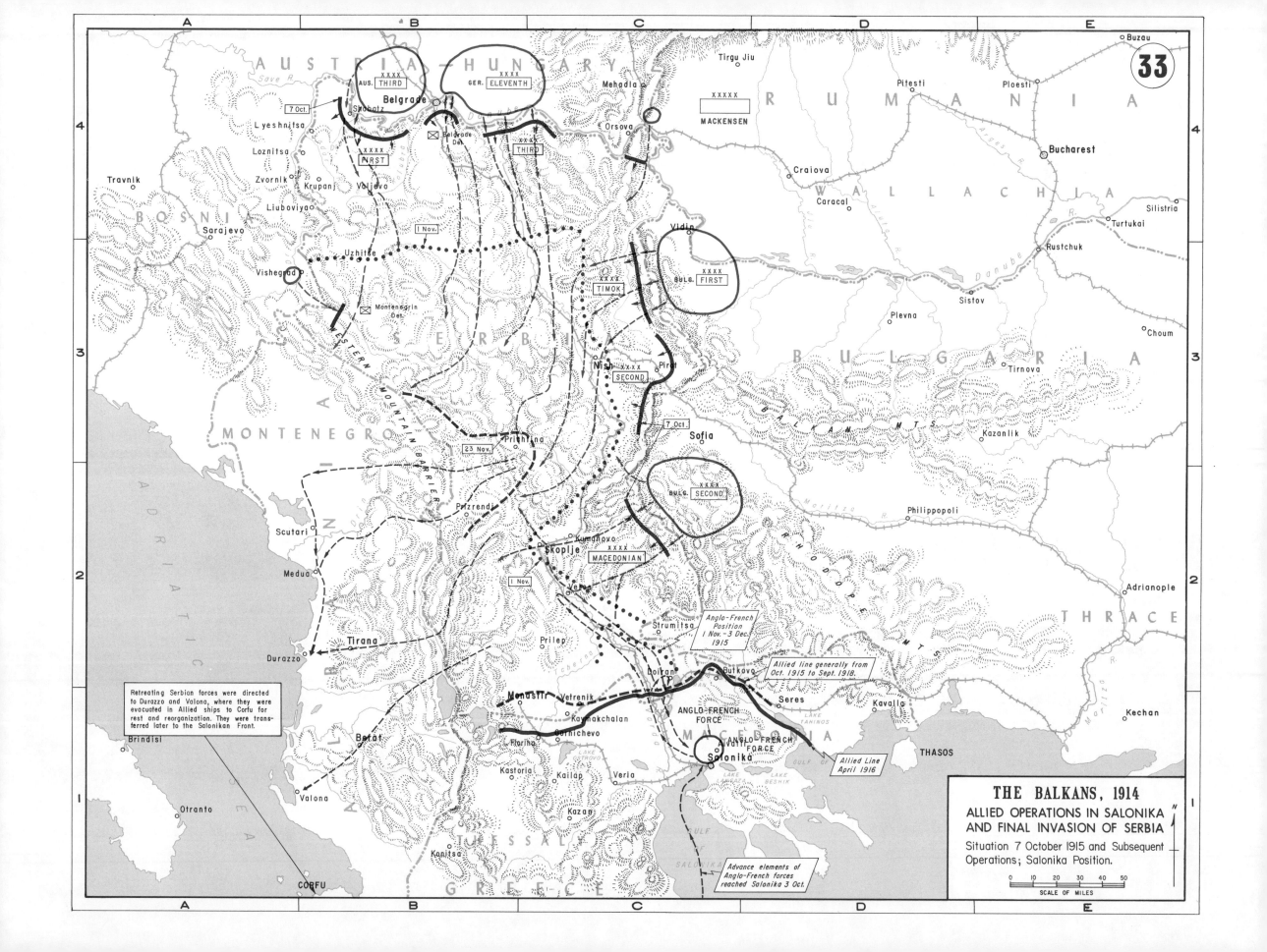

THE BALKANS, 1914
ALLIED OPERATIONS IN SALONIKA
AND FINAL INVASION OF SERBIA

Situation 7 October 1915 and Subsequent
Operations; Salonika Position.

Retreating Serbian forces were directed
to Durazzo and Valona, where they were
evacuated in Allied ships to Corfu for
rest and reorganization. They were transferred later to the Salonikan Front.

Advance elements of
Anglo-French forces
reached Salonika 3 Oct.

Allied Line
April 1916

Allied line generally from
Oct. 1915 to Sept. 1918.

Anglo-French Position
1 Nov. – 3 Dec.
1915

0 10 20 30 40 50
SCALE OF MILES

33

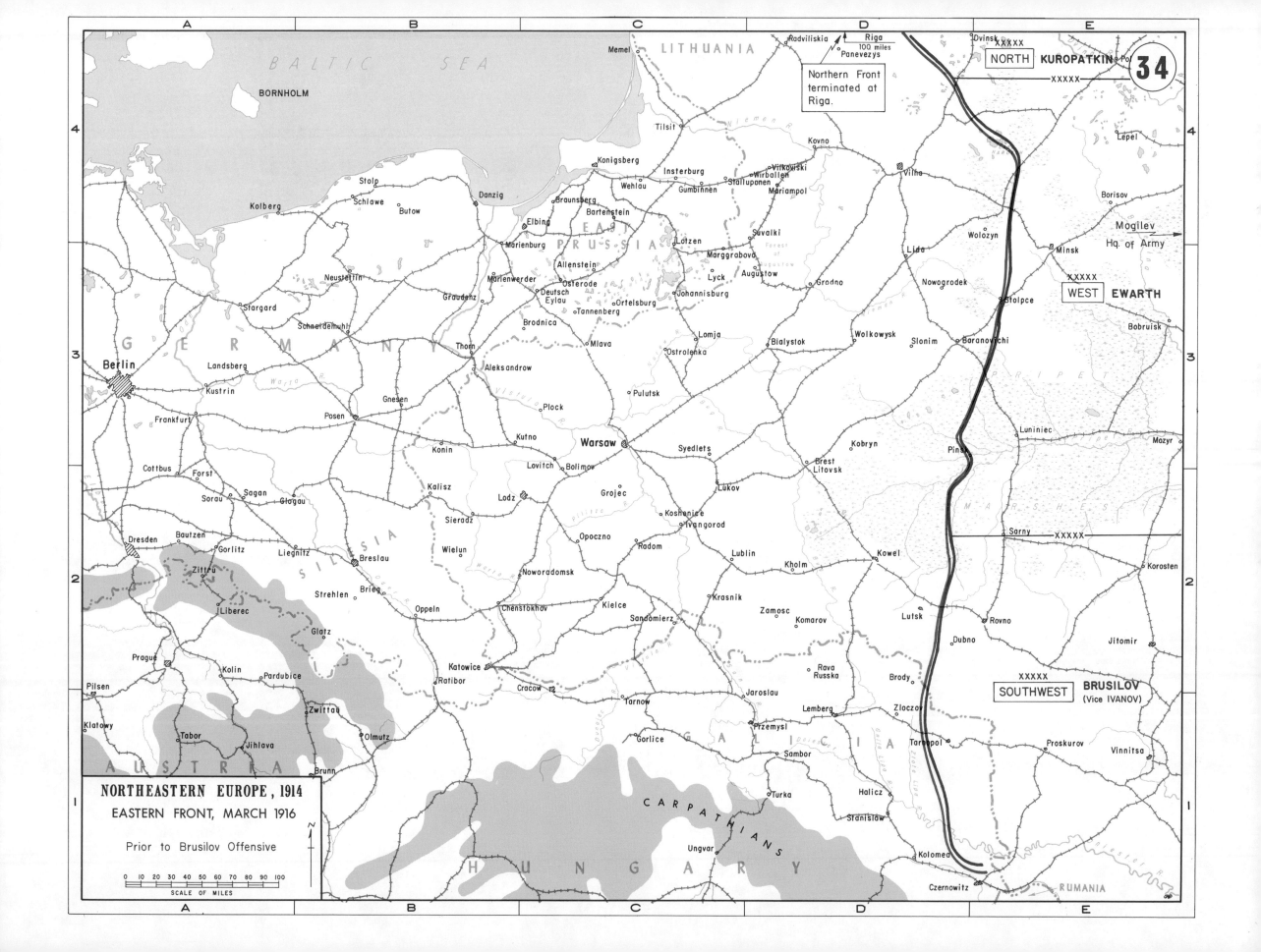

BALTIC SEA

BORNHOLM

LITHUANIA

Riga
100 miles
Panevezys

Northern Front terminated at Riga.

XXXXX
NORTH KUROPATKIN

34

Memel

Tilsit

Dvinsk

Lepel

Kovno

Vilha

Borisov

Stolp

Schlawe

Konigsberg

Insterburg

Vitkovski
Wirballen
Stalluponen
Mariampol

Mogilev
Hq. of Army

Kolberg

Butow

Danzig

Braunsberg
Bartenstein

Wehlau

Gumbinnen

Suvalki

Wolozyn

Minsk

Stargard

Neustettin

Marienburg
Elbing

EAST PRUSSIA

Lotzen

Marggrabova

Lida

Nowogrodek

Stolpce

WEST EWARTH

Landsberg

Schneidemuhl

Graudenz

Marienwerder
Deutsch Eylau
Osterode

Allenstein

Lyck
Augustow

Grodno

Wolkowysk

Slonim

Baranovichi

Bobruisk

Berlin

Kustrin

Frankfurt

GERMANY

Thorn

Brodnica

Tannenberg
Ortelsburg

Johannisburg

Lomja

Bialystok

PRIPET

Gnesen

Aleksandrow

Mlava

Ostrolenka

Pulutsk

Luniniec

Mozyr

Posen

Plock

Warsaw

Syedlets

Brest Litovsk

Kobryn

Pinsk

Sarny

XXXXX

Korosten

Konin

Kutno

Lovitch
Bolimov

Lukov

MARSHES

Cottbus

Forst

Sagan

Sorau

Glogau

Kalisz

Sieradz

Lodz

Grojec

Koshenice
Ivangorod

Kowel

Dresden
Bautzen

Gorlitz

Liegnitz

Breslau

Brieg

Wielun

Opoczno

Radom

Lublin

Kholm

Lutsk

Rovno

Jitomir

Zittau

Liberec

Strehlen

Oppeln

SILESIA

Noworadomsk

Chenstokhov

Kielce

Krasnik

Zamosc

Komarov

Brody

Dubno

Glatz

Prague

Kolin

Pardubice

Katowice
Ratibor

Sandomierz

Rava Russka

Zloczov

Proskurov

Vinnitsa

Pilsen

Klatowy

Tabor

Jihlava

Olmutz

Brunn

Zwittau

Cracow

Tarnow

Jaroslau

Lemberg

Przemysl

GALICIA

Tarnopol

SOUTHWEST BRUSILOV
(Vice IVANOV)

AUSTRIA

Gorlice

Sambor

Turka

Halicz

Stanislaw

CARPATHIANS

HUNGARY

Ungvar

Kolomea

Czernowitz

RUMANIA

NORTHEASTERN EUROPE, 1914
EASTERN FRONT, MARCH 1916
Prior to Brusilov Offensive

N

0 10 20 30 40 50 60 70 80 90 100
SCALE OF MILES

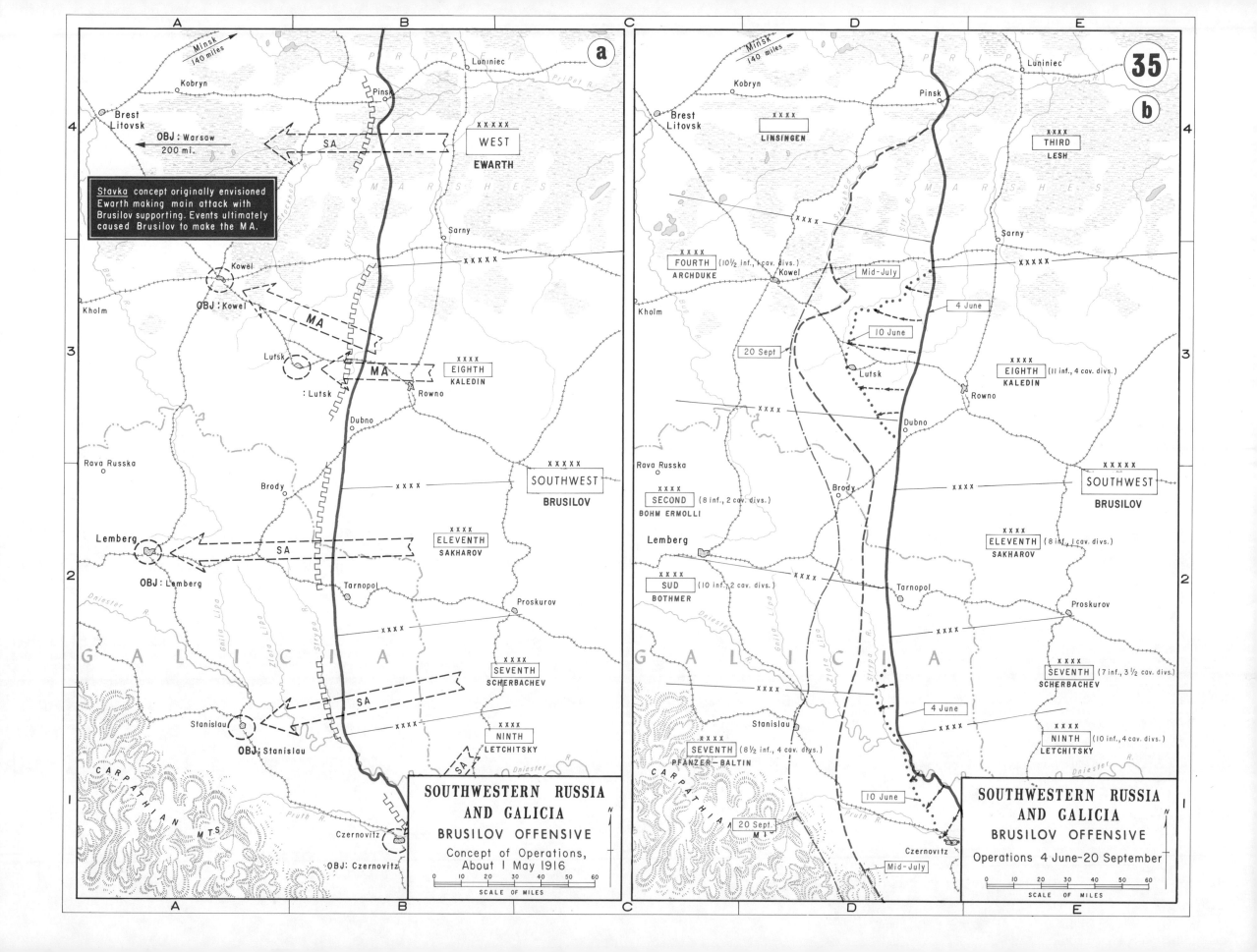

a

Minsk 140 miles

Luniniec

Kobryn

Pinsk

Brest Litovsk

OBJ: Warsaw 200 mi.

SA

XXXXX
WEST
EWARTH

Stavka concept originally envisioned Ewarth making main attack with Brusilov supporting. Events ultimately caused Brusilov to make the MA.

Sarny

Kowel

Kholm

OBJ: Kowel

MA

Lutsk

MA

: Lutsk

Rowno

XXXX
EIGHTH
KALEDIN

Dubno

Rava Russka

XXXXX
SOUTHWEST
BRUSILOV

Brody

XXXX

Lemberg

SA

XXXX
ELEVENTH
SAKHAROV

OBJ: Lemberg

Tarnopol

Proskurov

XXXX

G A L I C I A

XXXX
SEVENTH
SCHERBACHEV

Stanislau

SA

XXXX

XXXX
NINTH
LETCHITSKY

OBJ: Stanislau

SA

C A R P A T H I A N   M T S

Prut R.

Czernovitz

OBJ: Czernovitz

SOUTHWESTERN RUSSIA
AND GALICIA
BRUSILOV OFFENSIVE

Concept of Operations,
About 1 May 1916

N

0 10 20 30 40 50 60
SCALE OF MILES

b

35

Minsk 140 miles

Luniniec

Kobryn

Pinsk

Brest Litovsk

XXXX
LINSINGEN

XXXX
THIRD
LESH

XXXX

XXXX
FOURTH (10½ inf., 1 cav. divs.)
ARCHDUKE

Kowel

Mid-July

4 June

10 June

20 Sept

Sarny

XXXXX

Kholm

Lutsk

Rowno

XXXX
EIGHTH (11 inf., 4 cav. divs.)
KALEDIN

XXXX

Dubno

Rava Russka

XXXXX
SOUTHWEST
BRUSILOV

Brody

XXXX
SECOND (8 inf., 2 cav. divs.)
BOHM ERMOLLI

XXXX

Lemberg

XXXX
ELEVENTH (8 inf., 1 cav. divs.)
SAKHAROV

XXXX
SUD (10 inf., 2 cav. divs.)
BOTHMER

XXXX

Tarnopol

Proskurov

XXXX

G A L I C I A

XXXX

XXXX
SEVENTH (7 inf., 3½ cav. divs.)
SCHERBACHEV

4 June

Stanislau

XXXX

XXXX
NINTH (10 inf., 4 cav. divs.)
LETCHITSKY

XXXX
SEVENTH (8½ inf., 4 cav. divs.)
PFANZER–BALTIN

10 June

20 Sept

C A R P A T H I A N   M T S

Prut R.

Czernovitz

Mid-July

SOUTHWESTERN RUSSIA
AND GALICIA
BRUSILOV OFFENSIVE

Operations 4 June-20 September

N

0 10 20 30 40 50 60
SCALE OF MILES

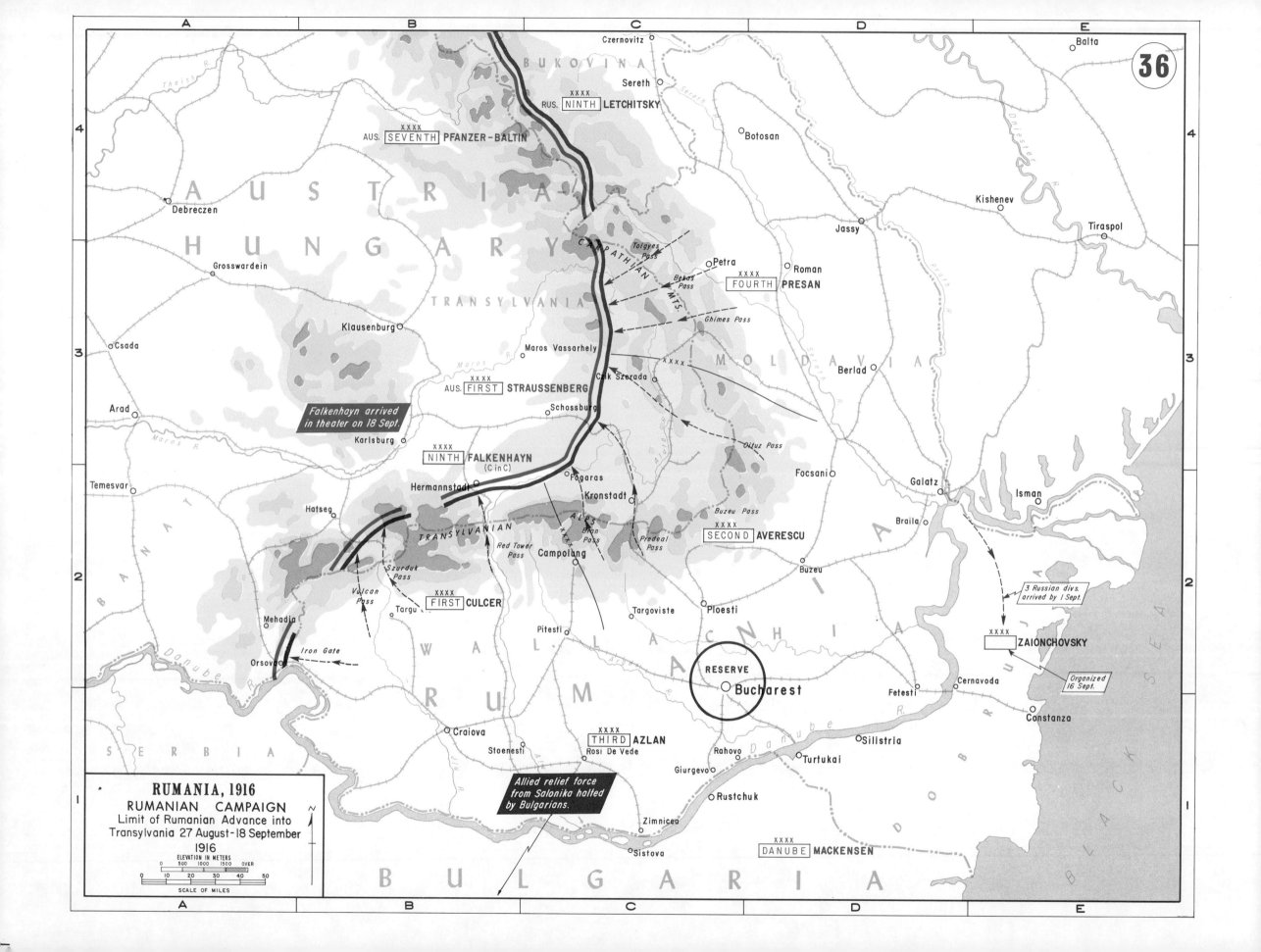

36

RUS. XXXX NINTH LETCHITSKY

AUS. XXXX SEVENTH PFANZER-BALTIN

BUKOVINA

Czernovitz
Sereth
Balta

Debreczen

Botosan

Kishenev

Tiraspol

Grosswardein

XXXX FOURTH PRESAN

Roman

Jassy

Petra

Tolgyes Pass

Bekas Pass

Ghimes Pass

TRANSYLVANIA

Klausenburg

Maros Vassarhely

XXXX MOLDAVIA

Berlad

Csada

Arad

AUS. XXXX FIRST STRAUSSENBERG

Csik Szereda

Schossburg

Oltuz Pass

Falkenhayn arrived in theater on 18 Sept.

Karlsburg

XXXX NINTH FALKENHAYN (C in C)

Focsani

Galatz

Isman

Temesvar

Hatseg

Hermannstadt

Fogaras

Kronstadt

Buzeu Pass

XXXX SECOND AVERESCU

Braila

TRANSYLVANIAN

Red Tower Pass

ALPS Bran Pass

Predeal Pass

Campolung

Szurduk Pass

Vulcan Pass

XXXX FIRST CULCER

Targu

Pitesti

Targoviste

Buzeu

Ploesti

3 Russian divs. arrived by 1 Sept.

Mehadia

Orsova

Iron Gate

WALLACHIA

XXXX ZAIONCHOVSKY

Organized 16 Sept.

RESERVE
Bucharest

Cernavoda

Fetesti

Constanza

SERBIA

Craiova

Stoenesti

XXXX THIRD AZLAN
Rosi De Vede

Rahovo

Giurgevo

Turtukai

Silistria

Rustchuk

Allied relief force from Salonika halted by Bulgarians.

Zimnicea

Sistova

XXXX DANUBE MACKENSEN

BULGARIA

BLACK SEA

RUMANIA, 1916
RUMANIAN CAMPAIGN
Limit of Rumanian Advance into
Transylvania 27 August-18 September
1916

ELEVATION IN METERS
500 1000 1500 OVER

0 10 20 30 40 50
SCALE OF MILES

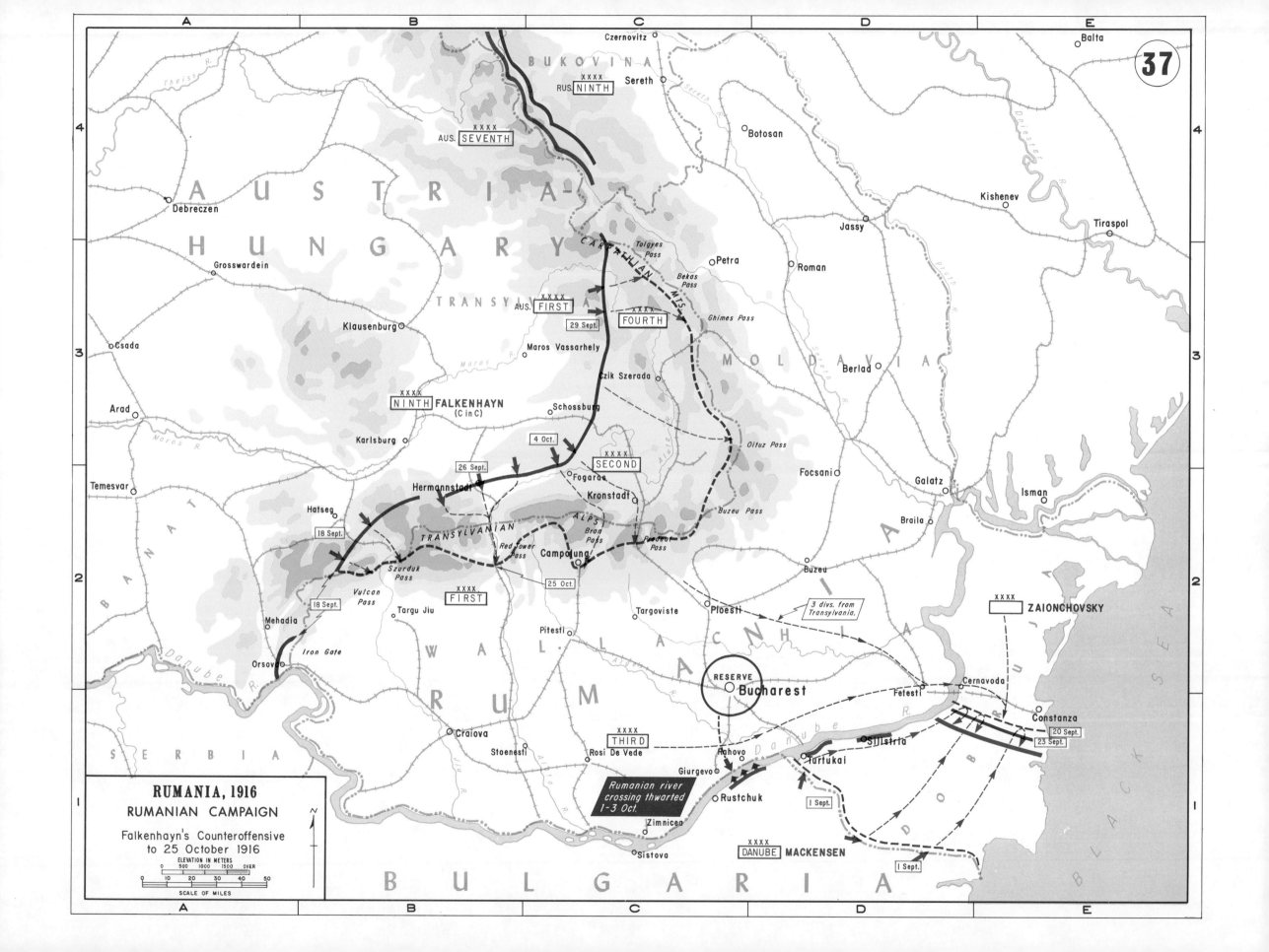

RUMANIA, 1916
RUMANIAN CAMPAIGN

Falkenhayn's Counteroffensive
to 25 October 1916

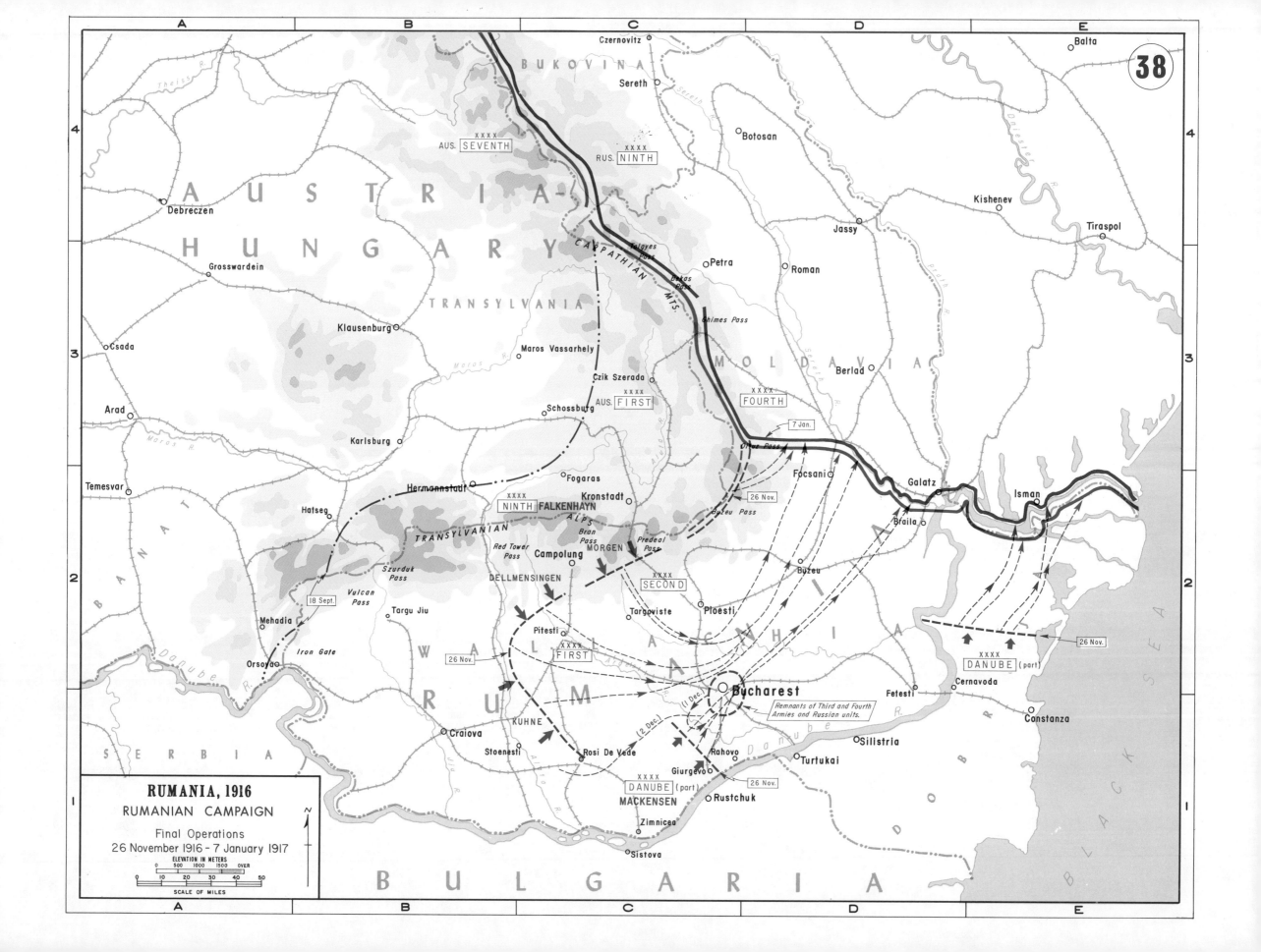

38

RUMANIA, 1916
RUMANIAN CAMPAIGN
Final Operations
26 November 1916 – 7 January 1917

ELEVATION IN METERS
500 1000 1500 OVER
10   20   30   40   50
SCALE OF MILES

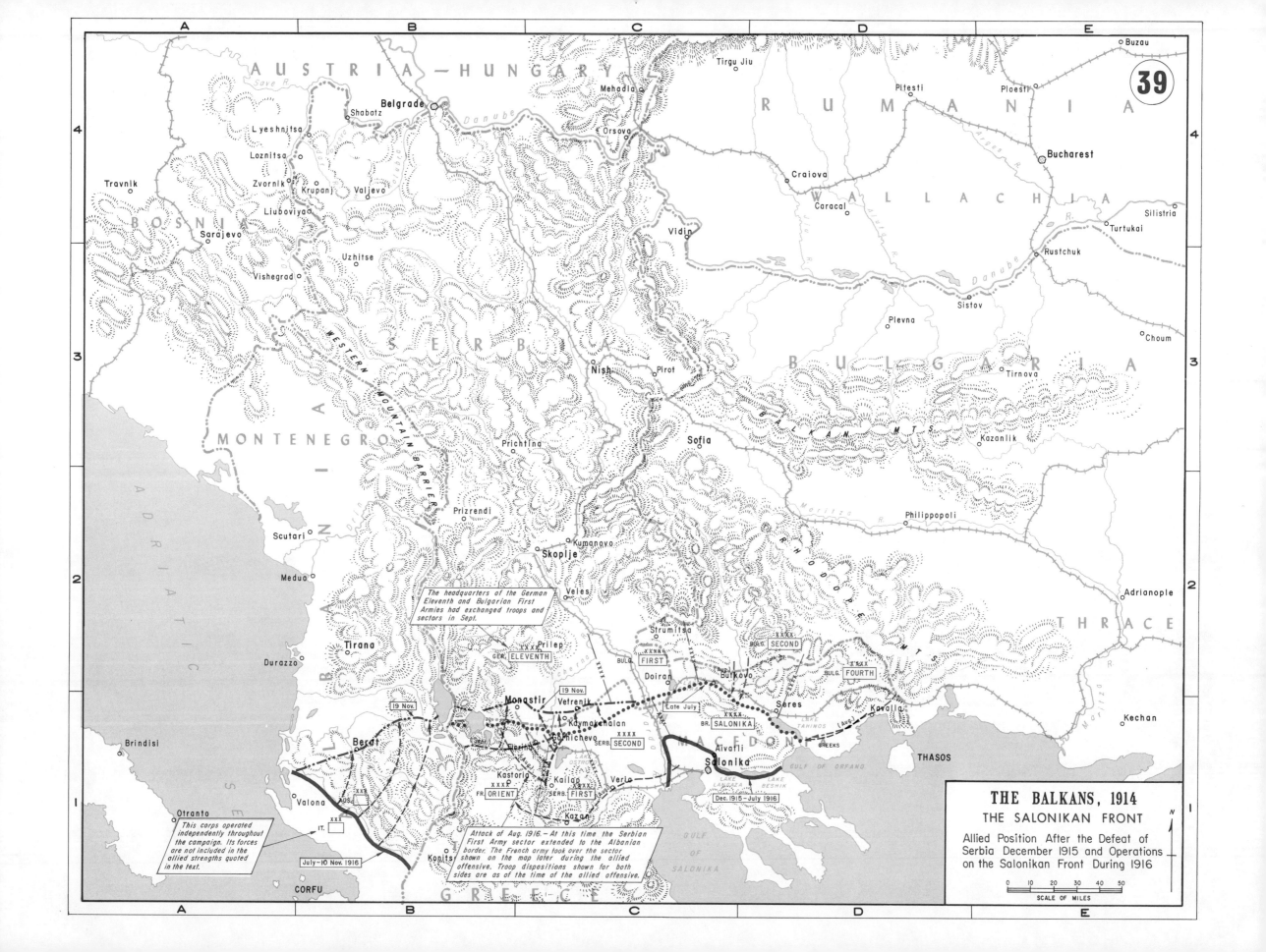

AUSTRIA — HUNGARY

RUMANIA

Buzau

Ploesti

Pitesti

WALLACHIA

Bucharest

BOSNIA

Travnik

Sarajevo

Vishegrad

Lyeshnjtsa

Loznitsa

Zvornik

Krupanj

Liubaviya

Uzhitse

Belgrade

Shabatz

Save R.

Danube

Valjevo

Mehadia

Orsova

Vidin

Craiova

Caracal

Silistria

Turtukai

Rustchuk

Danube

Sistov

Choum

MONTENEGRO

WESTERN MOUNTAIN BARRIER

SERBIA

Nish

Pirot

BULGARIA

Plevna

Sistov

Tirnova

BALKAN MTS.

Kazanlik

Scutari

Prizrendi

Prichtina

Sofia

RHODOPE MTS.

Philippopoli

Medua

ADRIATIC

Kumanovo

Skopije

Moritza R.

Adrianople

Tirana

Veles

THRACE

Durazzo

The headquarters of the German Eleventh and Bulgarian First Armies had exchanged troops and sectors in Sept.

Prilep

GER. ELEVENTH

Strumitsa

BULG. SECOND

BULG. FIRST

Doiran

Butkovo

BULG. FOURTH

Seres

Kavalla

19 Nov.

19 Nov.

Monastir

Vetrenik

Kaymakchalan

Late July

BR. SALONIKA

LAKE TAHINOS

Aug.

THASOS

Berat

Florina

Dobrichevo

SERB. SECOND

Aivarli

MACEDONIA

Salonika

GREEKS

Brindisi

Kastoria

Kailar

SERB. FIRST

Verla

GULF OF ORFANO

Kechan

Valona

FR. ORIENT

LAKE LANGAZA

LAKE BESHIK

Dec.1915–July 1916

This corps operated independently throughout the campaign. Its forces are not included in the allied strengths quoted in the text.

Otranto

IT.

Kazan

GULF OF SALONIKA

July–10 Nov. 1916

Konits

Attack of Aug. 1916.—At this time the Serbian First Army sector extended to the Albanian border. The French army took over the sector shown on the map later during the allied offensive. Troop dispositions shown for both sides are as of the time of the allied offensive.

CORFU

GREECE

39

THE BALKANS, 1914
THE SALONIKAN FRONT

Allied Position After the Defeat of
Serbia December 1915 and Operations
on the Salonikan Front During 1916

0 10 20 30 40 50
SCALE OF MILES

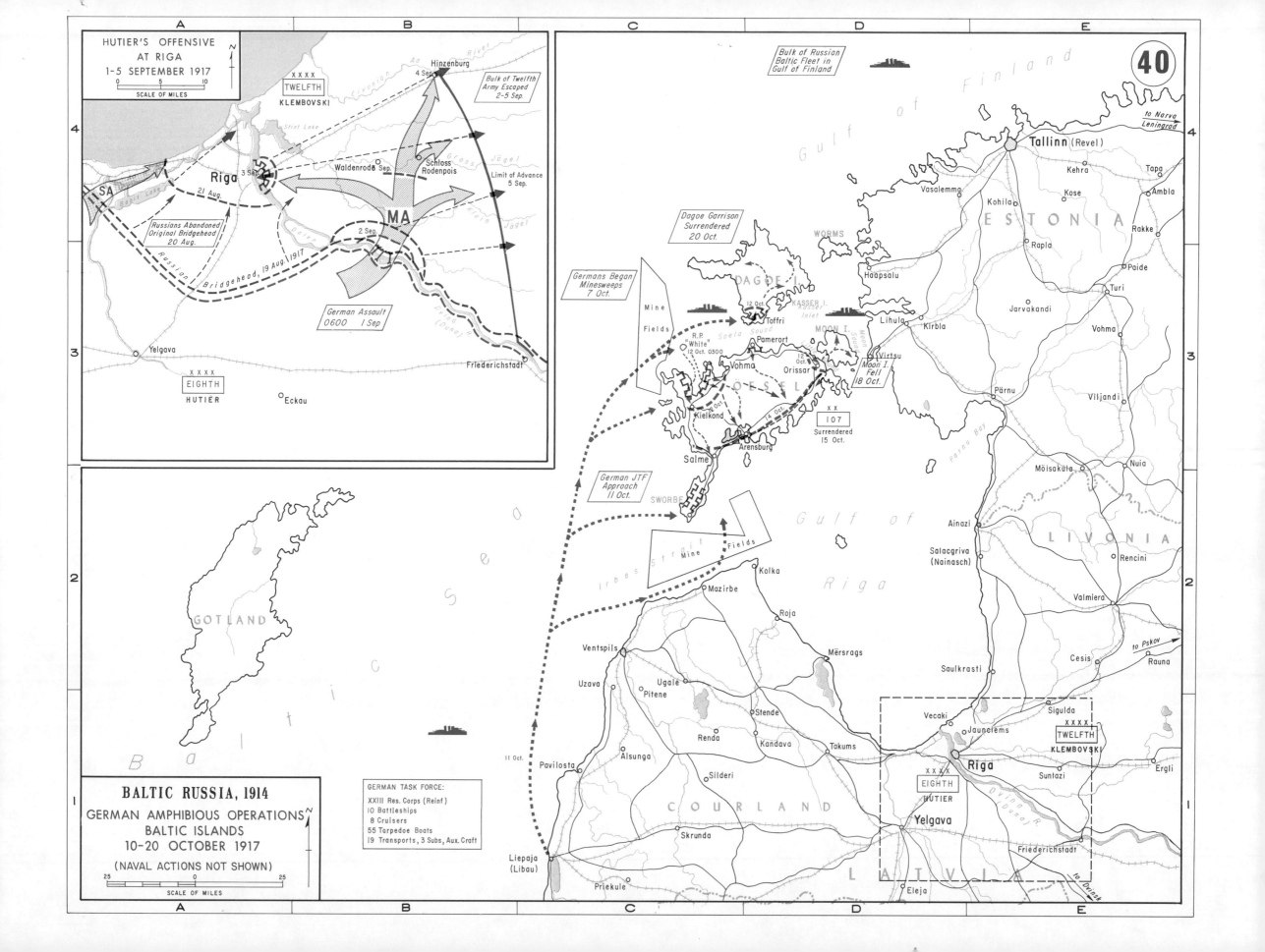

HUTIER'S OFFENSIVE AT RIGA
1-5 SEPTEMBER 1917

SCALE OF MILES
0   5   10

XXXX
TWELFTH
KLEMBOVSKI

Hinzenburg
4 Sep.

Bulk of Twelfth Army Escaped 2-5 Sep.

Riga 3 Sep.

Waldenrode Sep.

Schloss Rodenpois Sep.

Limit of Advance 5 Sep.

SA

21 Aug.

Russians Abandoned Original Bridgehead 20 Aug.

Russian Bridgehead, 19 Aug. 1917

MA

2 Sep.

German Assault 0600 1 Sep.

Yelgava

Friederichstadt

XXXX
EIGHTH
HUTIER

Eckau

Bulk of Russian Baltic Fleet in Gulf of Finland

Dagoe Garrison Surrendered 20 Oct.

DAGOE

Germans Began Minesweeps 7 Oct.

Mine Fields

R.P. "White" 12 Oct. 0300

Toffri

Pamerort

Vohma

KASSER I.

Kasser Inlet

MOON I.

Virtsu

Moon I. Fell 18 Oct.

ÖSEL

Orissar

Kielkond

14 Oct.

XX
107
Surrendered 15 Oct.

Arensburg

Salme

German JTF Approach 11 Oct.

SWORBE

Irbes Strait   Mine   Fields

Gulf of Finland

to Narva Leningrad

Tallinn (Revel)

Kehra

Tapa

Ambla

Rakke

Vasalemma

Kohila

Rapla

Paide

ESTONIA

Haapsalu

Lihula

Kirbla

Jarvakandi

Turi

Vohma

WORMS

Viljandi

Pärnu

Nuia

Mõisaküla

Pärnu Bay

Ainazi

Salacgriva (Nainasch)

Rencini

LIVONIA

Valmiera

to Pskov

Cesis

Rauna

Gulf of Riga

Kolka

Mazirbe

Roja

Mërsrags

Saulkrasti

Sigulda

XXXX
TWELFTH
KLEMBOVSKI

Ventspils

Uzava

Ugale

Pitene

Stende

Renda

Kandava

Takums

Silderi

Vecaki

Jaunciems

Riga

XXXX
EIGHTH
HUTIER

Suntazi

Ergli

GOTLAND

B a l t i c   S e a

Ö s e l

Alsunga

11 Oct.

Pavilosta

Skrunda

Yelgava

Friederichstadt

to Divinsk

COURLAND

LATVIA

Liepaja (Libau)

Priekule

Eleja

BALTIC RUSSIA, 1914
GERMAN AMPHIBIOUS OPERATIONS
BALTIC ISLANDS
10-20 OCTOBER 1917

(NAVAL ACTIONS NOT SHOWN)

25   0   25
SCALE OF MILES

GERMAN TASK FORCE:
XXIII Res. Corps (Reinf)
10 Battleships
8 Cruisers
55 Torpedo Boats
19 Transports, 3 Subs, Aux. Craft

40

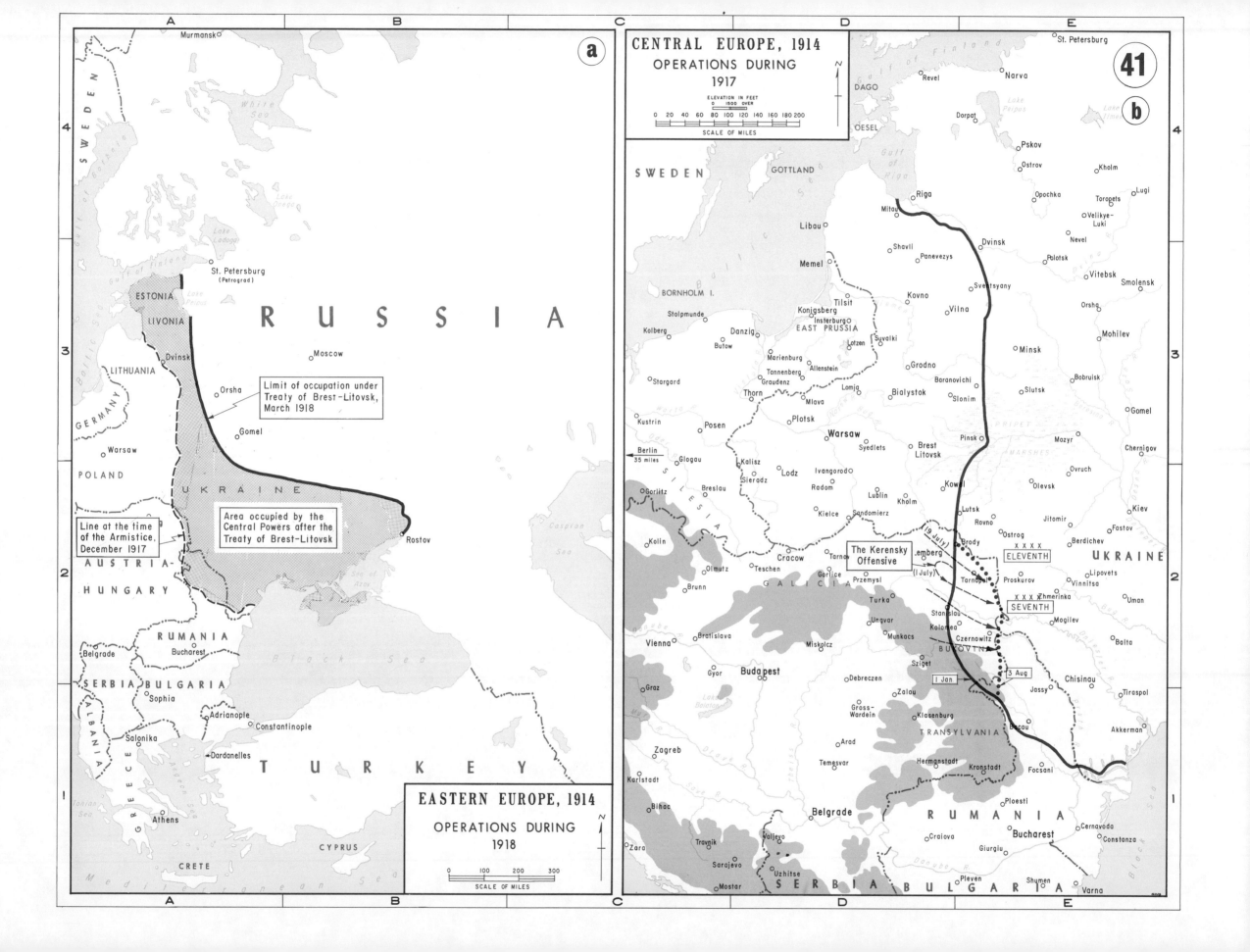

EASTERN EUROPE, 1914

OPERATIONS DURING
1918

SCALE OF MILES

CENTRAL EUROPE, 1914

OPERATIONS DURING
1917

ELEVATION IN FEET

SCALE OF MILES

41

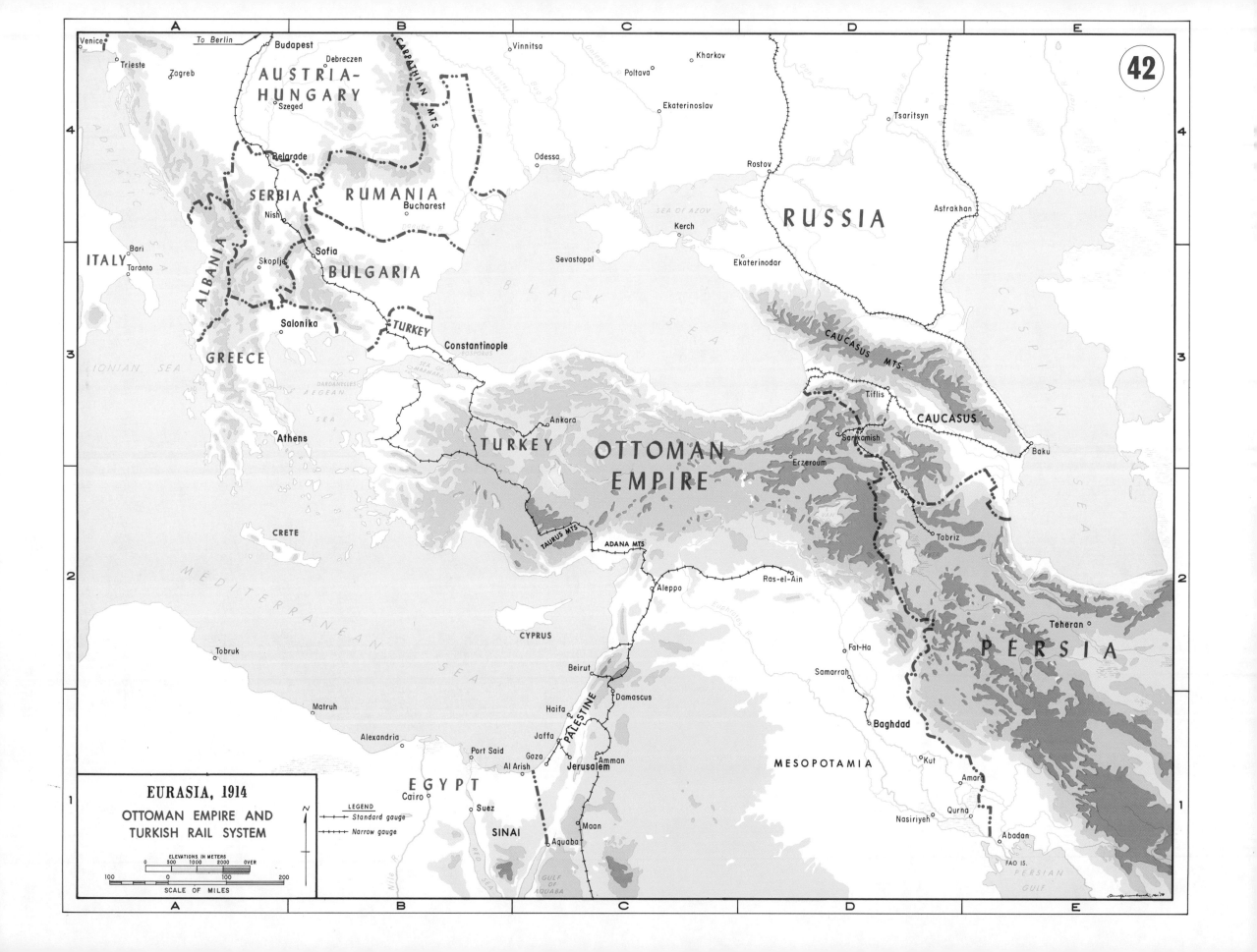

EURASIA, 1914
OTTOMAN EMPIRE AND
TURKISH RAIL SYSTEM

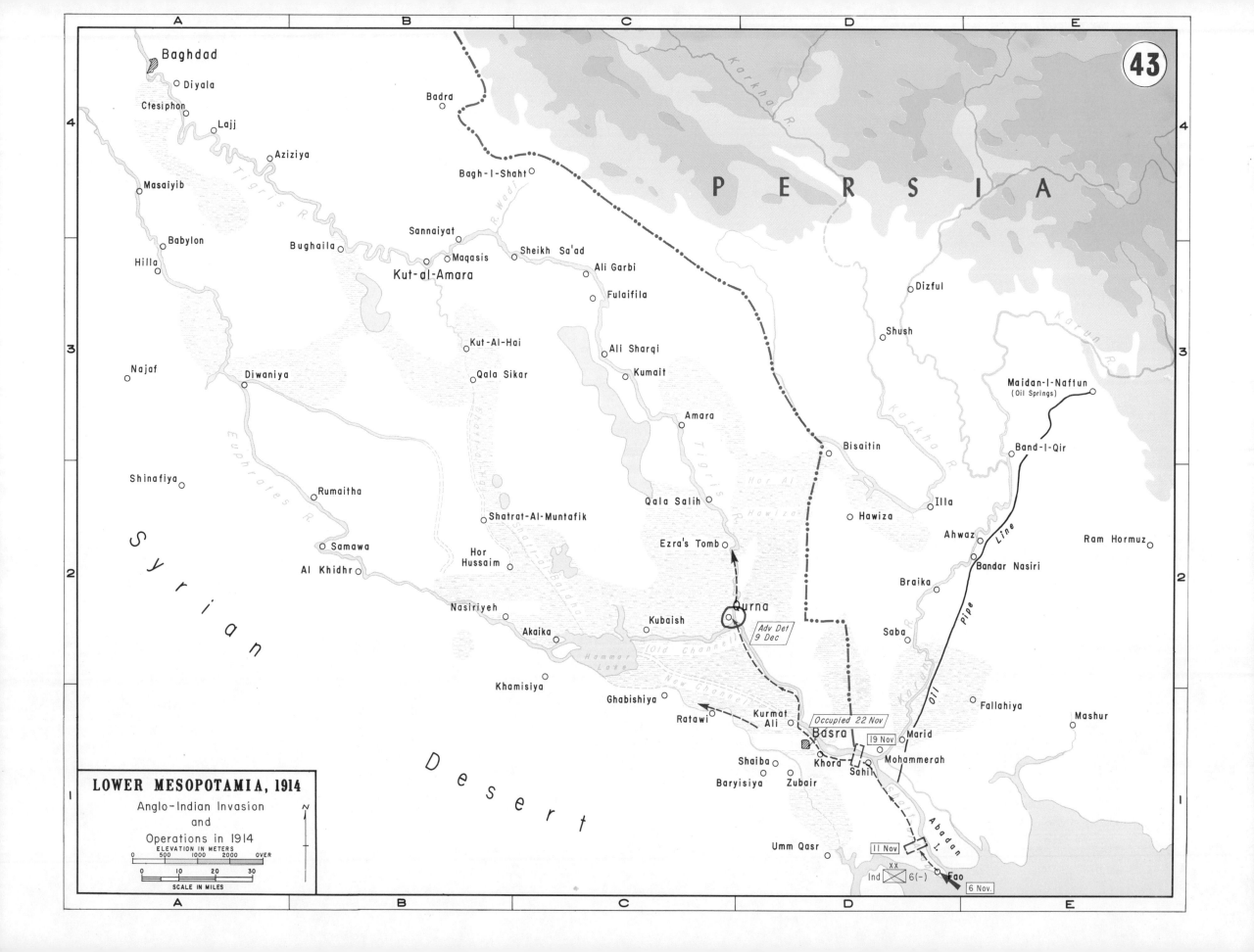

LOWER MESOPOTAMIA, 1914

Anglo-Indian Invasion
and
Operations in 1914

ELEVATION IN METERS
0   500 1000 2000 OVER

0   10   20   30
SCALE IN MILES

43

P E R S I A

S y r i a n

D e s e r t

Baghdad
Diyala
Ctesiphon
Lajj
Aziziya
Masaiyib
Babylon
Hilla
Najaf
Shinafiya

Badra
Bagh-I-Shaht
Sannaiyat
Bughaila
Maqasis
Kut-al-Amara
Sheikh Sa'ad
Ali Garbi
Fulaifila
Kut-Al-Hai
Qala Sikar
Ali Sharqi
Kumait
Diwaniya
Rumaitha
Amara
Shatrat-Al-Muntafik
Ali Sharqi
Qala Salih
Hor Al Hawiza
Samawa
Hor Hussaim
Ezra's Tomb
Al Khidhr
Nasiriyeh
Kubaish
Qurna
Adv Det 9 Dec
Akaika
Khamisiya
Ghabishiya
Ratawi
Kurmat Ali
Occupied 22 Nov
Basra
19 Nov
Shaiba
Khord
Baryisiya
Zubair
Sahil
Umm Qasr
11 Nov
Ind XX 6(-) Fao
6 Nov.

Dizful
Shush
Maidan-I-Naftun
(Oil Springs)
Bisaitin
Band-I-Qir
Hawiza
Illa
Ahwaz
Ram Hormuz
Bandar Nasiri
Braika
Saba
Fallahiya
Mashur
Marid
Mohammerah
Abadan I.

Tigris R.
Euphrates R.
Karkha R.
Karun R.
Shatt-al-Arab
Oil Pipe Line
Hammar Lake
(Old Channel)
New Channel

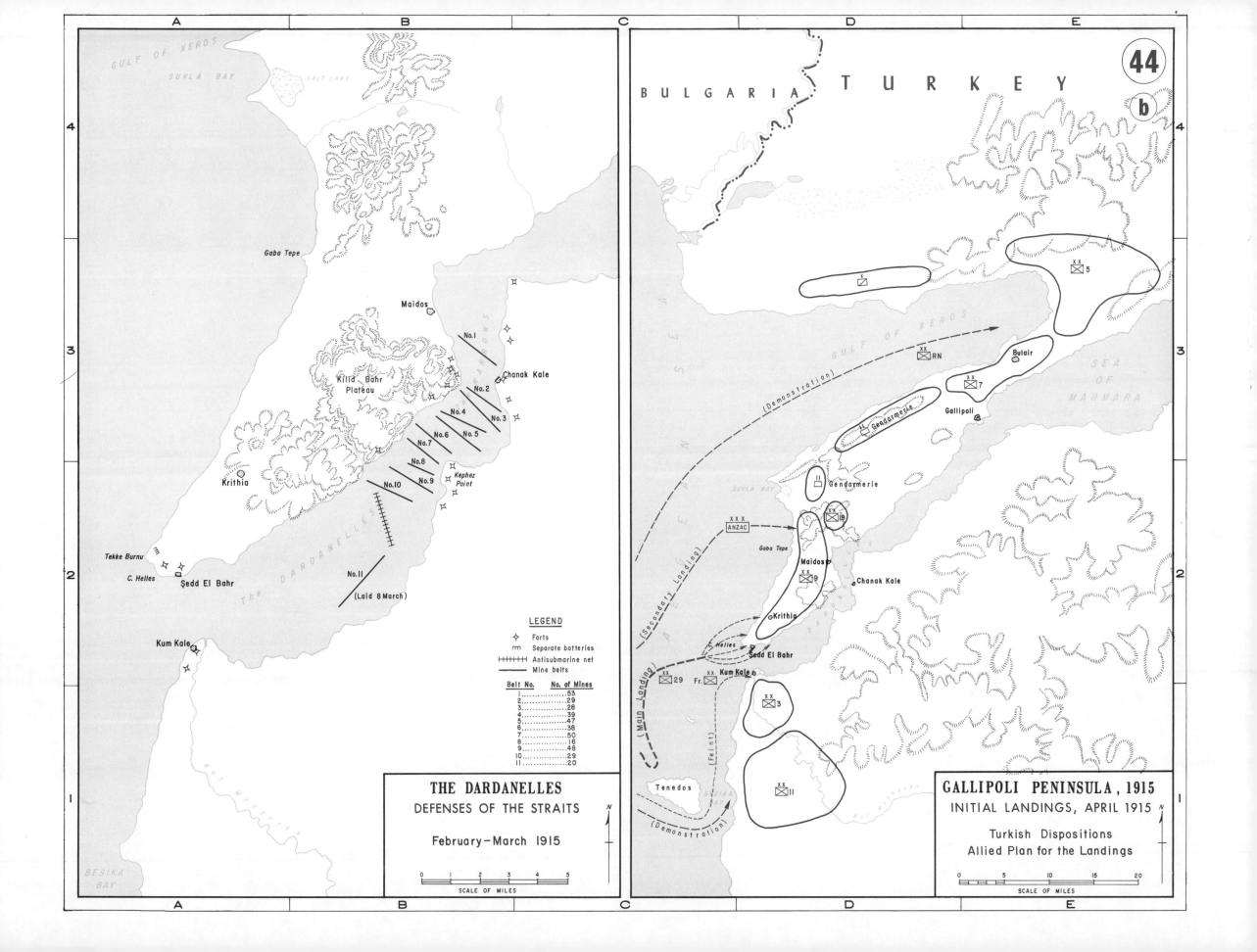

THE DARDANELLES

DEFENSES OF THE STRAITS

February—March 1915

LEGEND

✦ Forts
⊓⊓ Separate batteries
┼┼┼┼ Antisubmarine net
── Mine belts

Belt No.	No. of Mines
1	53
2	29
3	28
4	39
5	47
6	38
7	50
8	16
9	48
10	29
11	20

SCALE OF MILES
0 1 2 3 4 5

N

GALLIPOLI PENINSULA, 1915

INITIAL LANDINGS, APRIL 1915

Turkish Dispositions
Allied Plan for the Landings

SCALE OF MILES
0 5 10 15 20

N

44
b

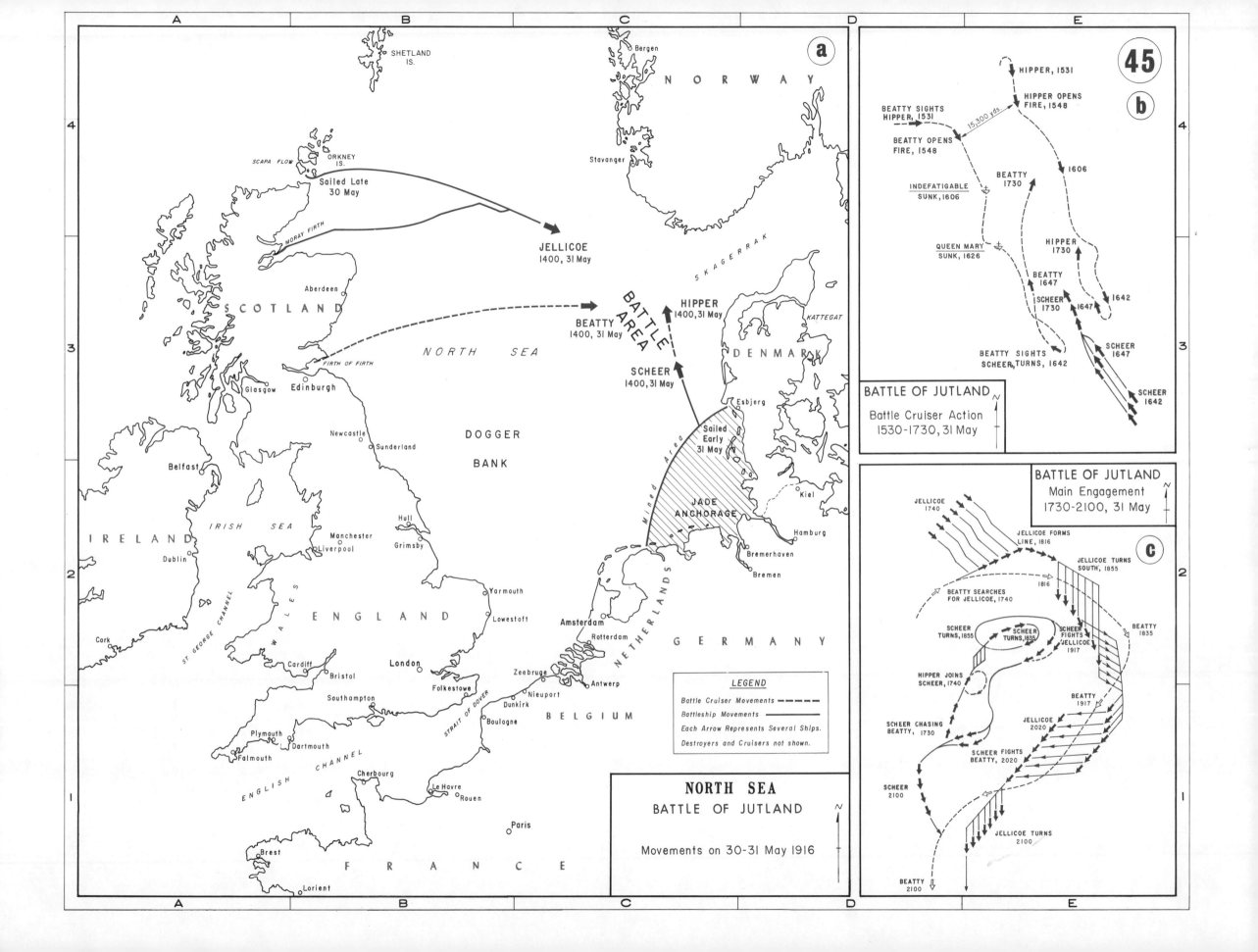

a

SHETLAND IS.

NORWAY

Bergen

Stavanger

SCAPA FLOW
ORKNEY IS.
Sailed Late 30 May

MORAY FIRTH

JELLICOE
1400, 31 May

SCOTLAND

Aberdeen

SKAGERRAK

BATTLE AREA

HIPPER
1400, 31 May

BEATTY
1400, 31 May

DENMARK

KATTEGAT

Glasgow

Edinburgh

FIRTH OF FIRTH

NORTH SEA

SCHEER
1400, 31 May

Esbjerg

Newcastle

Sunderland

DOGGER BANK

Sailed Early 31 May

Mined Area

Kiel

IRELAND

IRISH SEA

Belfast

Hull

Grimsby

JADE ANCHORAGE

Hamburg

Bremerhaven

Dublin

Manchester

Liverpool

Bremen

Yarmouth

WALES

ENGLAND

Lowestoft

NETHERLANDS

GERMANY

Cork

ST GEORGE CHANNEL

Amsterdam

Rotterdam

Cardiff

Bristol

London

Zeebruge

Antwerp

Southampton

Folkestowe

Nieuport

Dunkirk

BELGIUM

Plymouth

Dartmouth

ENGLISH CHANNEL

STRAIT OF DOVER

Boulogne

LEGEND

Battle Cruiser Movements - - - -

Battleship Movements ———

Each Arrow Represents Several Ships.

Destroyers and Cruisers not shown.

Falmouth

Cherbourg

Le Havre

Rouen

NORTH SEA

BATTLE OF JUTLAND

Brest

Paris

Movements on 30-31 May 1916

FRANCE

Lorient

b

45

HIPPER, 1531

HIPPER OPENS FIRE, 1548

BEATTY SIGHTS HIPPER, 1531

15,300 yds.

BEATTY OPENS FIRE, 1548

1606

BEATTY 1730

INDEFATIGABLE SUNK, 1606

HIPPER 1730

QUEEN MARY SUNK, 1626

BEATTY 1647

SCHEER 1730

1642

BEATTY SIGHTS SCHEER, TURNS, 1642

SCHEER 1647

SCHEER 1647

1647

SCHEER 1642

BATTLE OF JUTLAND

Battle Cruiser Action
1530-1730, 31 May

BATTLE OF JUTLAND

Main Engagement
1730-2100, 31 May

c

JELLICOE 1740

JELLICOE FORMS LINE, 1816

1816

JELLICOE TURNS SOUTH, 1855

BEATTY SEARCHES FOR JELLICOE, 1740

BEATTY 1835

SCHEER TURNS, 1855

SCHEER TURNS, 1835

SCHEER FIGHTS JELLICOE, 1917

HIPPER JOINS SCHEER, 1740

BEATTY 1917

SCHEER CHASING BEATTY, 1730

JELLICOE 2020

SCHEER FIGHTS BEATTY, 2020

SCHEER 2100

JELLICOE TURNS 2100

BEATTY 2100

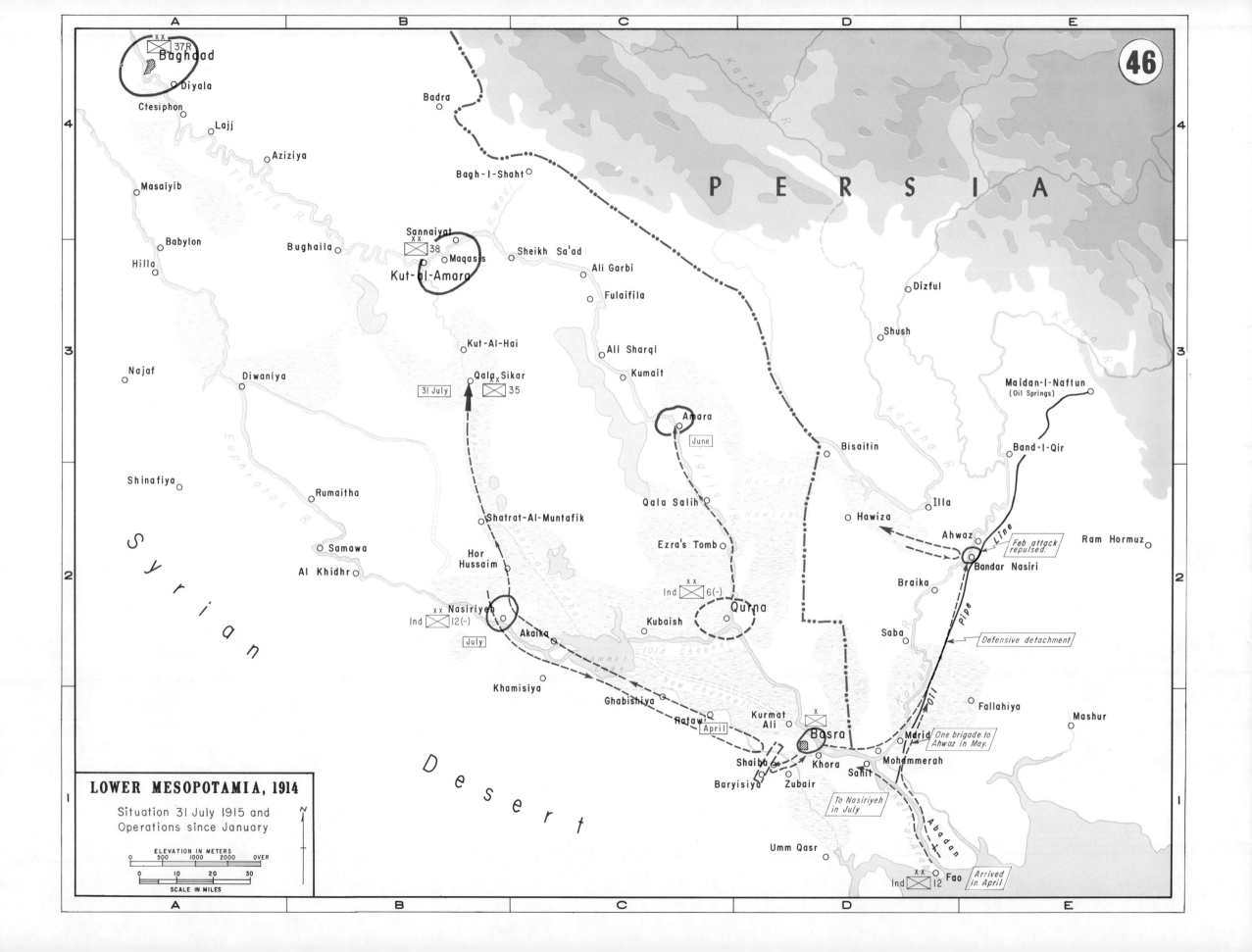

LOWER MESOPOTAMIA, 1914

Situation 31 July 1915 and
Operations since January

ELEVATION IN METERS
0 500 1000 2000 OVER

0 10 20 30
SCALE IN MILES

46

P E R S I A

S y r i a n

D e s e r t

Baghdad
XX 37R
Diyala
Ctesiphon
Lajj
Aziziya
Masaiyib
Badra
Bagh-I-Shaht
Babylon
Bughaila
Hilla
Sannaiyat
XX 38
Maqasis
Sheikh Sa'ad
Kut-al-Amara
Ali Garbi
Fulaifila
Najaf
Diwaniya
Kut-Al-Hai
Ali Sharqi
Qala Sikar
XX 35
31 July
Kumait
Shinafiya
Rumaitha
Amara
June
Bisaitin
Dizful
Shush
Maidan-I-Naftun
(Oil Springs)
Band-I-Qir
Shatrat-Al-Muntafik
Qala Salih
Hawiza
Ahwaz
Feb attack
repulsed.
Samawa
Hor
Hussaim
Ezra's Tomb
Illa
Ram Hormuz
Al Khidhr
Nasiriyeh
Ind 12(-)
July
Akaika
XX
Ind 6(-)
Qurna
Kubaish
Braika
Bandar Nasiri
Khamisiya
Saba
Defensive detachment
Ghabishiya
Ratawi
April
Kurmat
Ali
Basra
X
Mdrid
One brigade to
Ahwaz in May.
Fallahiya
Mashur
Shaiba
Khora
Baryisiya
Zubair
Sahit
Mohammerah
To Nasiriyeh
in July
Umm Qasr
Abadan
Ind 12
Fao
Arrived
in April

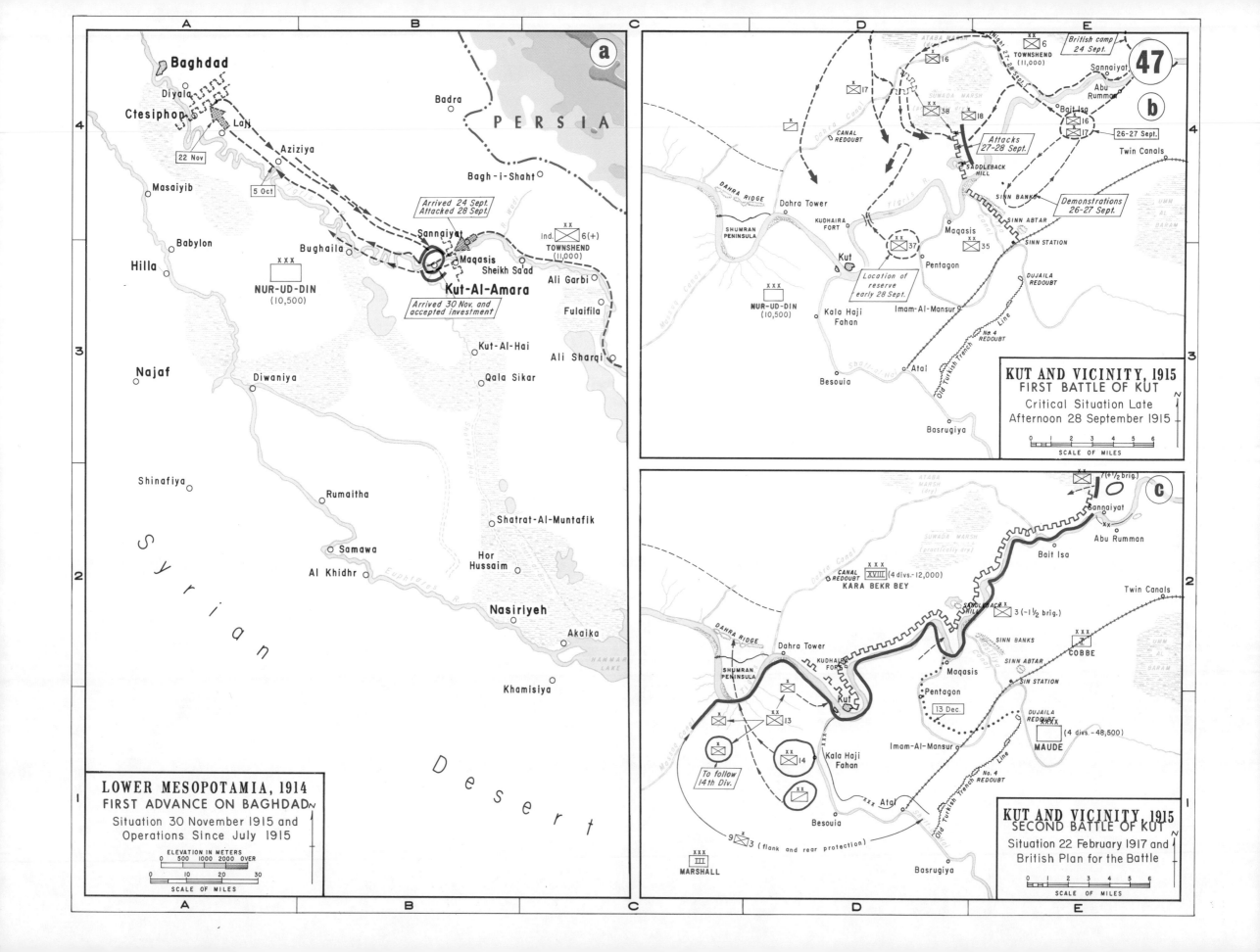

a

Baghdad

Diyala
Ctesiphon
Laij

PERSIA

Badra

22 Nov

Aziziya

5 Oct

Masaiyib

Bagh-i-Shaht

Babylon

Arrived 24 Sept.
Attacked 28 Sept.

Hilla

Bughaila
Sannaiyat

NUR-UD-DIN
(10,500)

Ind. XX 6(+)
TOWNSHEND
(11,000)

Maqasis
Sheikh Sa'ad

Kut-Al-Amara

Ali Garbi

Arrived 30 Nov. and
accepted investment

Fulaifila

Najaf

Diwaniya

Kut-Al-Hai

Qala Sikar

Ali Sharqi

Shinafiya

Rumaitha

Shatrat-Al-Muntafik

Samawa

Al Khidhr

Hor
Hussaim

Nasiriyeh

Akaika

HAMMAR
LAKE

Khamisiya

S y r i a n

D e s e r t

Euphrates R.

LOWER MESOPOTAMIA, 1914
FIRST ADVANCE ON BAGHDAD
Situation 30 November 1915 and
Operations Since July 1915

ELEVATION IN METERS
0 500 1000 2000 OVER

0   10   20   30
SCALE OF MILES

b

47

XX 6

XX 16

TOWNSHEND
(11,000)

British camp
24 Sept.

Sannaiyat

X 17

X 38

X 18

Abu
Rumman

Bait Isa

XX 16

Attacks
27-28 Sept.

XX 17

26-27 Sept.

X

CANAL
REDOUBT

ATABA MARSH

SUWADA MARSH

SADDLEBACK
HILL

SINN BANKS

Twin Canals

DAHRA RIDGE

Dahra Tower

KUDHAIRA
FORT

SINN ABTAR

Demonstrations
26-27 Sept.

SINN STATION

SHUMRAN
PENINSULA

Kut

XX 37

Maqasis

XX 35

UMM
AL
BARAM

Pentagon

Imam-Al-Mansur

DUJAILA
REDOUBT

NUR-UD-DIN
(10,500)

Location of
reserve
early 28 Sept.

Kala Haji
Fahan

Old Turkish Trench Line

No. 4
REDOUBT

Besouia

Atal

Basrugiya

KUT AND VICINITY, 1915
FIRST BATTLE OF KUT
Critical Situation Late
Afternoon 28 September 1915

0 1 2 3 4 5 6
SCALE OF MILES

c

XX 7(+½ brig.)

Sannaiyat

ATABA
MARSH
(dry)

XX

Abu Rumman

Bait Isa

SUWADA MARSH
(practically dry)

XXX XVIII (4 divs.-12,000)
CANAL
REDOUBT
KARA BEKR BEY

SADDLEBACK
HILL

XX 3 (-1½ brig.)

SINN BANKS

XXX
COBBE

Twin Canals

DAHRA RIDGE

Dahra Tower

KUDHAIRA
FORT

SINN ABTAR

SIN STATION

UMM
AL
BARAM

SHUMRAN
PENINSULA

Maqasis

13 Dec.

DAHRA Canal

Kut

Pentagon

DUJAILA
REDOUBT
XXXX (4 divs.-48,500)
MAUDE

X

XX 13

Imam-Al-Mansur

XX

XX 14

Kala Haji
Fahan

Old Turkish Trench Line

No. 4
REDOUBT

To follow
14th Div.

Besouia

Atal

9 XX 3 (flank and rear protection)

XXX
III
MARSHALL

Basrugiya

KUT AND VICINITY, 1915
SECOND BATTLE OF KUT
Situation 22 February 1917 and
British Plan for the Battle

0 1 2 3 4 5 6
SCALE OF MILES

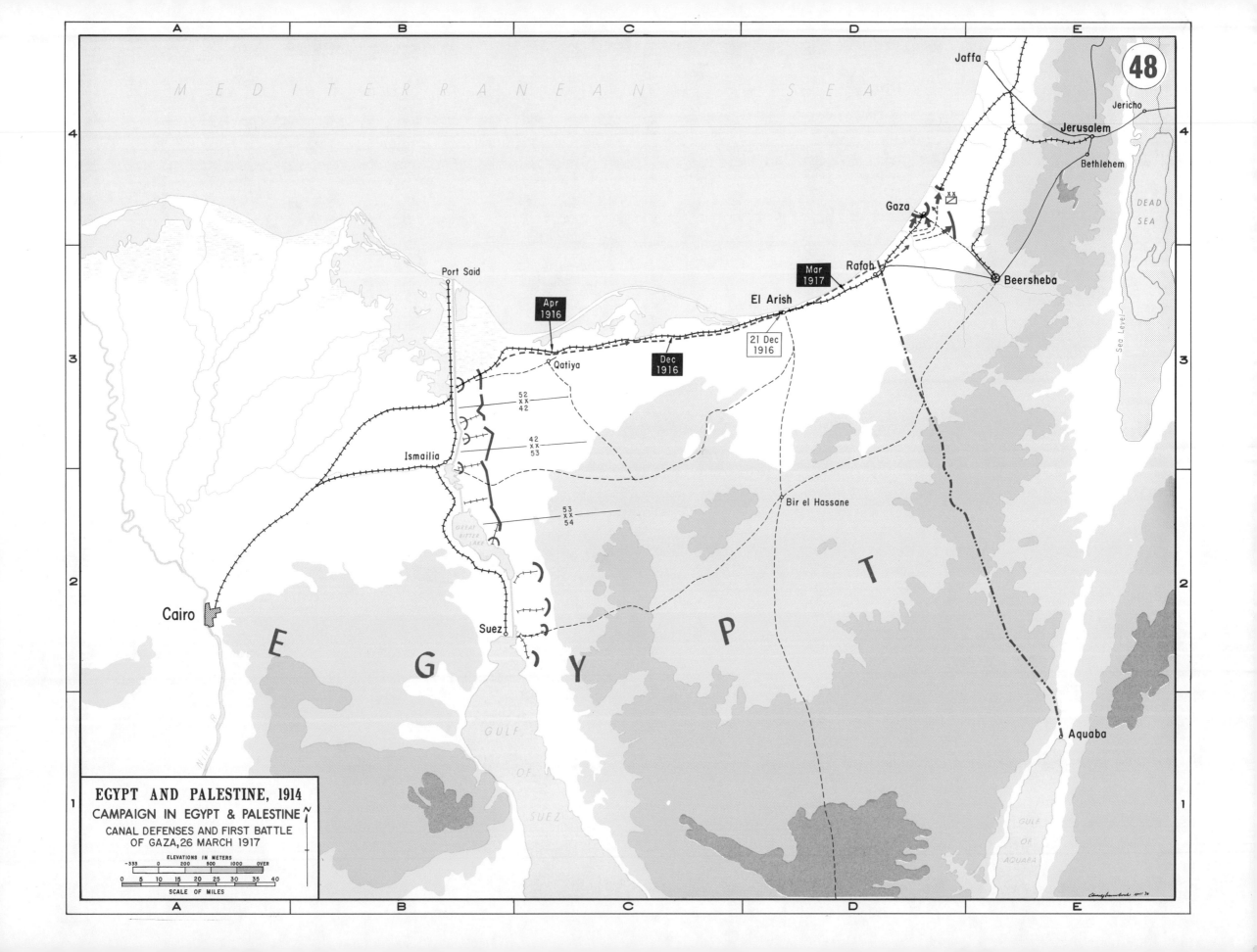

48

MEDITERRANEAN SEA

Jaffa

Jerusalem

Jericho

Bethlehem

DEAD SEA

Gaza

Mar 1917   Rafah

Beersheba

Port Said

El Arish

Apr 1916

21 Dec 1916

Qatiya

Dec 1916

52
XX
42

42
XX
53

Ismailia

53
XX
54

GREAT BITTER LAKE

Bir el Hassane

Cairo

NILE RIVER

E   G   Y   P   T

Suez

GULF OF SUEZ

Aquaba

GULF OF AQUABA

Sea Level

EGYPT AND PALESTINE, 1914
CAMPAIGN IN EGYPT & PALESTINE
CANAL DEFENSES AND FIRST BATTLE
OF GAZA, 26 MARCH 1917

ELEVATIONS IN METERS
-333   200   500   1000   OVER

0   5   10   15   20   25   30   35   40
SCALE OF MILES

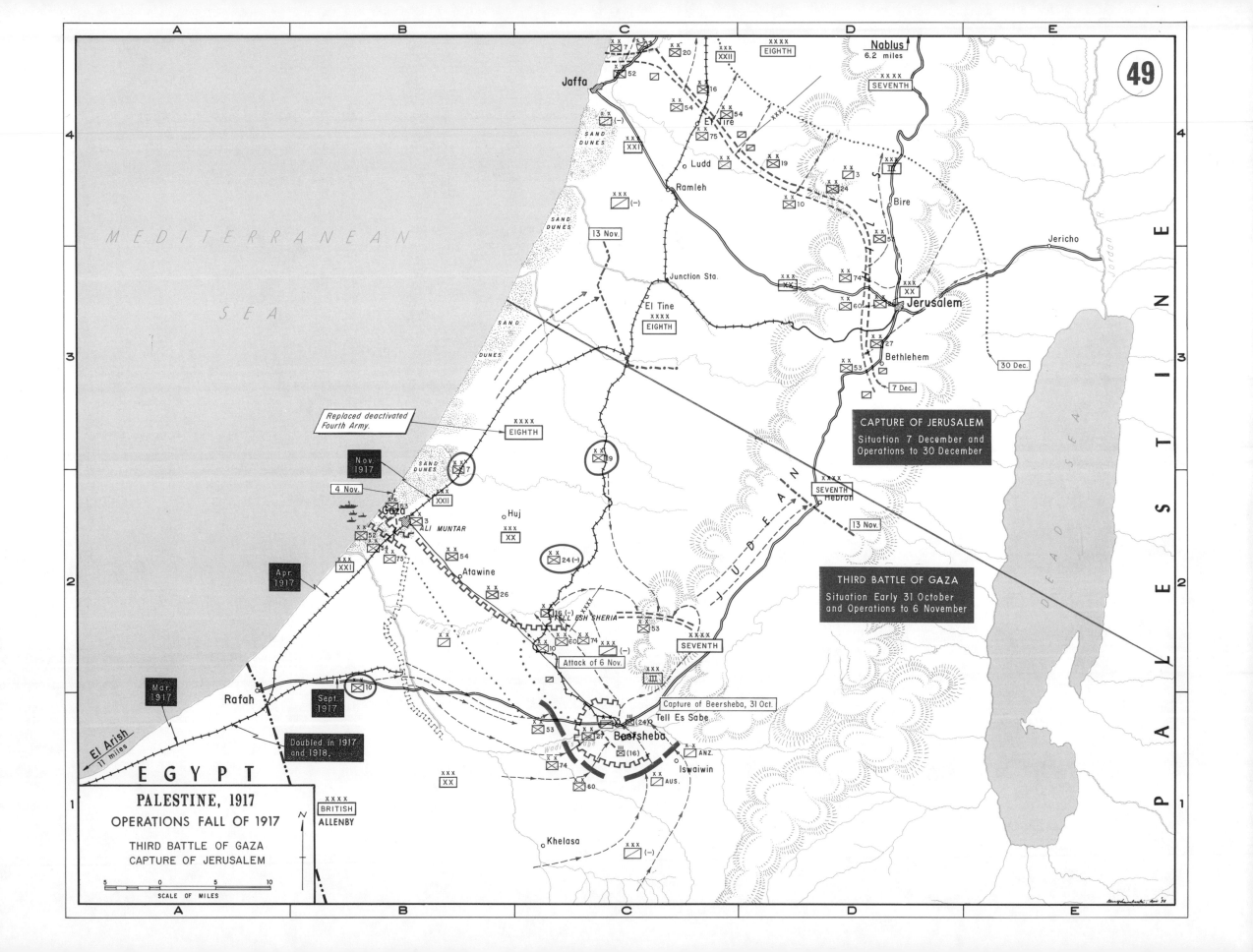

MEDITERRANEAN SEA

Nablus
6.2 miles

Jaffa

El Tire

Ludd

Ramleh

Jericho

Junction Sta.

El Tine
XXXX
EIGHTH

Jerusalem

Bethlehem

30 Dec.

7 Dec.

Replaced deactivated
Fourth Army.

XXXX
EIGHTH

CAPTURE OF JERUSALEM
Situation 7 December and
Operations to 30 December

Nov.
1917

4 Nov.

Gaza

ALI MUNTAR

Huj

Hebron

13 Nov.

Atawine

THIRD BATTLE OF GAZA
Situation Early 31 October
and Operations to 6 November

Apr.
1917

TELL ESH SHERIA

SEVENTH

Attack of 6 Nov.

Mar.
1917

Rafah

Sept.
1917

Capture of Beersheba, 31 Oct.

Tell Es Sabe

El Arish
11 miles

Doubled in 1917
and 1918.

EGYPT

Beersheba

Iswaiwin

ANZ.

AUS.

Khelasa

PALESTINE, 1917
OPERATIONS FALL OF 1917

THIRD BATTLE OF GAZA
CAPTURE OF JERUSALEM

XXXX
BRITISH
ALLENBY

N

5   0   5   10
SCALE OF MILES

49

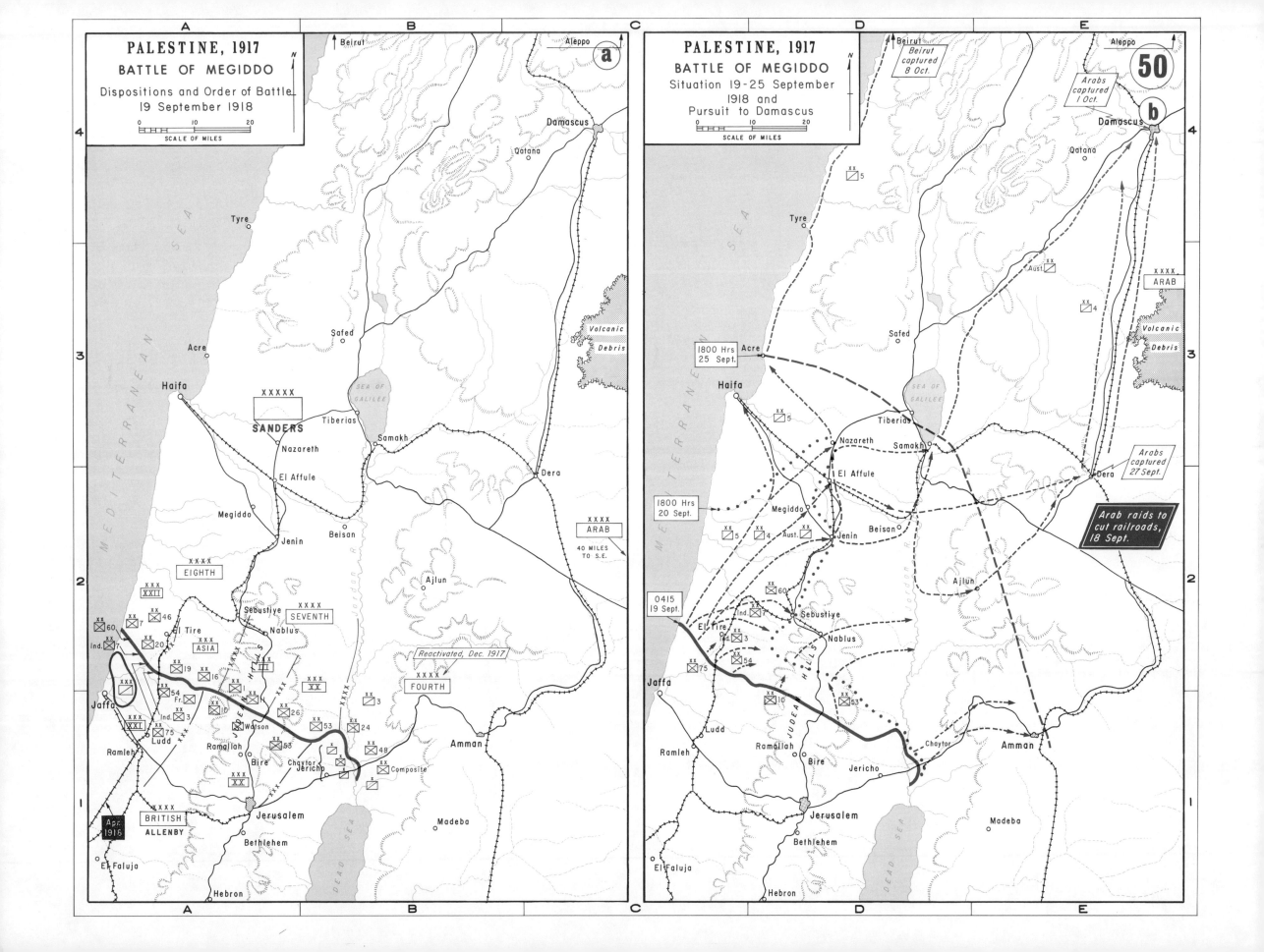

PALESTINE, 1917

BATTLE OF MEGIDDO

Dispositions and Order of Battle
19 September 1918

SCALE OF MILES
0   10   20

a

Beirut
Aleppo
Damascus
Qatana
Tyre
Safed
Acre
Haifa
Volcanic Debris
SEA OF GALILEE
Tiberias
XXXXX
SANDERS
Samakh
Nazareth
Dera
El Affule
Megiddo
Beisan
Jenin
XXXX
ARAB
40 MILES TO S.E.
XXXX
EIGHTH
XXX XXII
XXX 46
XX 60
XX 7
El Tire
XXX 20
Sebustiye
XXXX
SEVENTH
Nablus
Ind. XX 7
XXX ASIA
XX 19
XX 16
III
XX 1
XX 54 Fr.
XX 10
XXX
XX 26
XXX XX
XX 3
Jaffa
Ind. XX 3
Watson
XX 53
XX 24
Reactivated, Dec. 1917
XXX XXI
XX 75
Ludd
Ramleh
Ramallah
XX 53
Chaytor
XX 48
Composite
XXXX
FOURTH
Bire
Jericho
XX
Amman
Apr. 1918
XXXX
BRITISH
ALLENBY
Jerusalem
Madeba
Bethlehem
El Faluja
Hebron
DEAD SEA

PALESTINE, 1917

BATTLE OF MEGIDDO

Situation 19-25 September
1918 and
Pursuit to Damascus

SCALE OF MILES
0   10   20

50

b

Beirut _captured 8 Oct._
Aleppo
Damascus
Arabs captured 1 Oct.
Qatana
XX 5
Tyre
Aust. XX
Safed
XX 4
XXXX
ARAB
Volcanic Debris
1800 Hrs 25 Sept. Acre
Haifa
SEA OF GALILEE
XX 5
Tiberias
Samakh
Nazareth
Dera
Arabs captured 27 Sept.
1800 Hrs 20 Sept.
El Affule
Megiddo
Beisan
XX 5   XX 4   Aust. XX
Jenin
Ajlun
Arab raids to cut railroads, 18 Sept.
0415 19 Sept.
XX 60
Ind. XX 7
Sebustiye
El Tire
XX 3
Nablus
XX 54
XX 75
XX 10
XX 53
Jaffa
Ludd
Ramleh
Ramallah
Bire
Jericho
Chaytor
Amman
Jerusalem
Madeba
Bethlehem
El Faluja
Hebron
DEAD SEA

MEDITERRANEAN SEA

Jordan R.

JUDEA HILLS

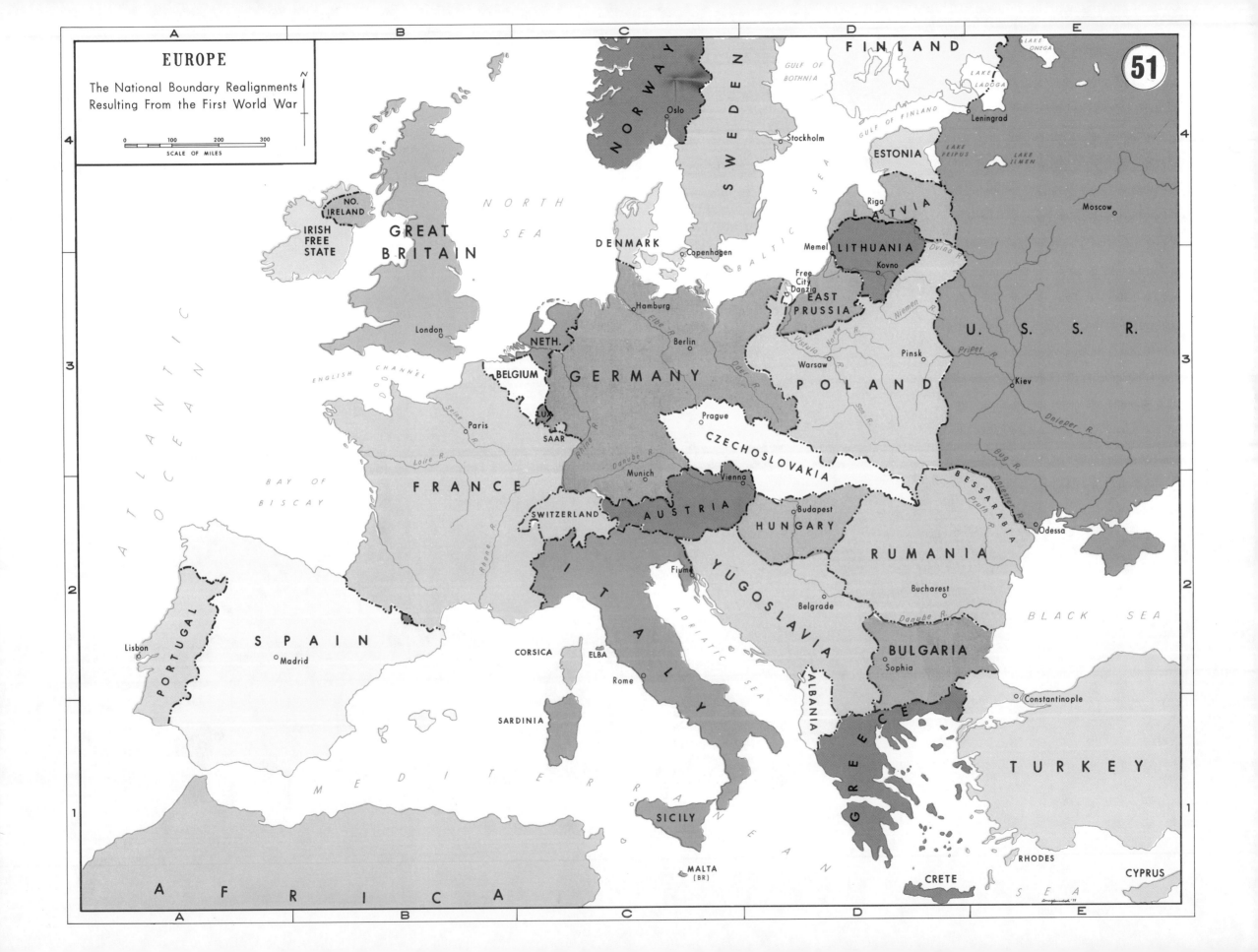

EUROPE

The National Boundary Realignments
Resulting From the First World War

0   100   200   300
SCALE OF MILES

FINLAND

LAKE ONEGA

LAKE LADOGA

NORWAY

Oslo

SWEDEN

Stockholm

GULF OF BOTHNIA

GULF OF FINLAND

Leningrad

LAKE ILMEN

ESTONIA

LAKE PEIPUS

Moscow

NORTH SEA

NO. IRELAND

IRISH FREE STATE

GREAT BRITAIN

DENMARK

Copenhagen

BALTIC SEA

Riga

LATVIA

Memel

LITHUANIA

Kovno

Dvina R.

Free City Danzig

EAST PRUSSIA

Niemen R.

U. S. S. R.

London

Hamburg

NETH.

Elbe R.

Berlin

Oder R.

Vistula R.

Bug R.

Warsaw

Pinsk

Pripet R.

Kiev

BELGIUM

GERMANY

POLAND

ENGLISH CHANNEL

LUX.

SAAR

Paris

Seine R.

Rhine R.

Prague

CZECHOSLOVAKIA

San R.

Dnieper R.

Loire R.

FRANCE

Munich

Danube R.

Vienna

AUSTRIA

HUNGARY

Budapest

BESSARABIA

Dniester R.

Pruth R.

Odessa

ATLANTIC OCEAN

BAY OF BISCAY

SWITZERLAND

Rhone R.

RUMANIA

Fiume

YUGOSLAVIA

Bucharest

PORTUGAL

SPAIN

ITALY

ADRIATIC SEA

Belgrade

Danube R.

BLACK SEA

Lisbon

Madrid

CORSICA

ELBA

Rome

SARDINIA

ALBANIA

BULGARIA

Sophia

Constantinople

GREECE

TURKEY

MEDITERRANEAN SEA

MALTA (BR)

SICILY

CRETE

RHODES

CYPRUS

AFRICA

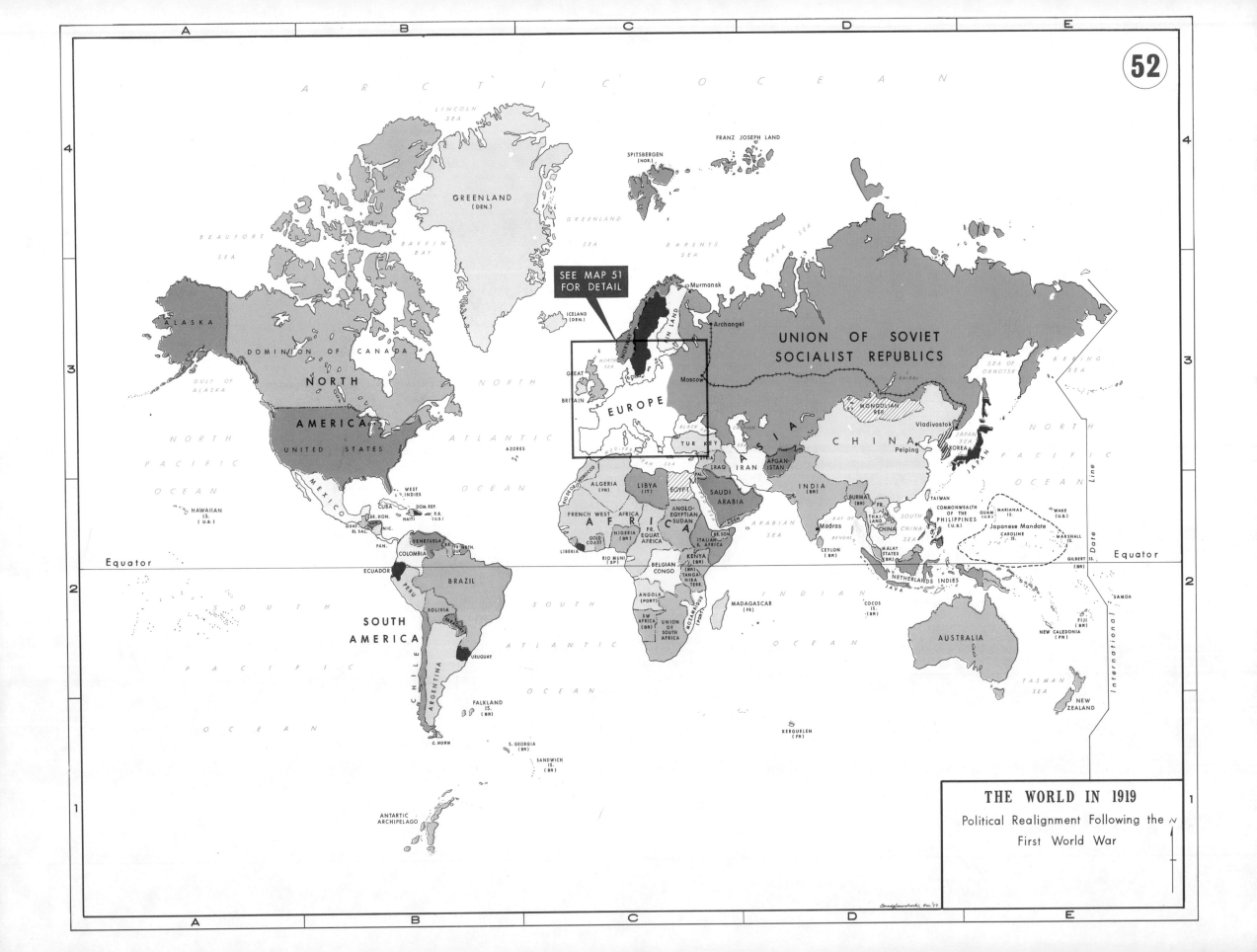

THE WORLD IN 1919

Political Realignment Following the First World War